900 GENIE

Maria Corven

Table of Contents

Chapter 1

As if hindered by the might of an angry deity, a desert sandstorm whipped around an unprotected caravan. Its victims rushed to and fro in a futile effort to safeguard their goods while frightened camels resisted their lead. The unyielding wind drowned their cries and with each ferocious roar, caused further damage to their supplies.

By afternoon, hours later, the Arab travelers had broken down their caravan into an acceptable camp. With the animals calmed, secured, and no longer in a terrified frenzy to escape, they erected tents and began to assess the damages from the storm while the unforgiving sun mercilessly cast its glare over their covered heads. The majority of their goods appeared unharmed, allowing them to differentiate the ruined from the salvageable, but the caravan wouldn't move again until they made necessary repairs.

Idris, the camel boy who tended to their herd, crossed the dunes for privacy to relieve himself. Dirt and filth clung to his once white, sweat-stained garments. Exhausted, he barely noticed the hint of red protruding from the sand.

"Huh... What's that?" He crouched to pull on the red fabric, fearing some item had been blown from their supplies. "Hey! I found something!" Idris cried out.

The men rushed toward him with their knives in hand. They probed the ground with their feet and used their weapon hilts to move the sand until the caravan leader motioned for them to step back. Hassan Ibn Museyr, a man known for his courage and stubborn work ethic, took over the dangerous role. A forgotten item in the sands of the desert could be anything.

"Hamid! Ali! See what we have here," Hassan ordered. "Careful!"

"This place is cursed," Ophir protested.

"Maybe it's a trap," Hamid said. He hung back initially, a reluctant expression on his bearded face. They were all worn and exhausted from their travels and few of them held anything but distrust for the mysterious object beneath the sand. They could be uncovering anything, and in the desert, there would be no one there to help them if their venture proved to have deadly consequences.

Hassan shot him a dark look that prompted Hamid to quickly join him. Hamid and Ali dug while the rest of the men stood by with their knives handy. They made signs against evil and shuddered. For their leader, they would obey as told, but they didn't like it.

Eventually, the shape of a short, stocky man emerged from the sand. His motionless body was half-clothed in dirty khaki pants and tattered red shirt. He didn't seem to be alive at first glance, a likely casualty of the recent storm.

"Is he alive?" Hassan asked.

Hamid bent over and pressed his ear against the man's hairy chest. After a moment he sat up and nodded. "His heart beats."

Hassan frowned. "Search him, he may be armed." The man had the look of an American, and too often, they came bearing ill will or meant to cause trouble.

Their thorough search turned up a keyring, wallet, an English-Arabic dictionary, a crumpled map, and a small revolver.

"Randy Connor," Ali read off the ID in the cracked, brown leather wallet. "From America."

"An infidel! As suspected!" Ophir spit on the sand and reached for the heavy, golden chain on the unconscious man's chest.

"Wait!" Hassan cried. "Allah is merciful. Even to the lowest who do not see his light. Give this man water. We must allow him to recover then determine the best course of action."

Disappointed, Ophir removed his waterskin and placed it to the stranger's lips. He was wise enough to only allow a few droplets to trickle out at a time, until the clear rivulets ran down his dirty, unshaven cheek. Immediately, the cool refreshment seemed to stir him from his unconscious state. The man dragged in a rasping breath of fresh air, preceding a coughing fit.

"He will bring nothing but trouble," Ophir grumbled in warning.

"You do not know that," Hassan replied. "Take him to the tent."

They dragged the coughing man away to the camp.

***

An enormous, silver moon hung over the horizon in a cloudless, star-filled sky. Overcome with exhaustion, the

Arabs surrounded the fire to recuperate. Their animals lay resting while Idris slumbered nearby.

Randy, their disgruntled survivor found in the sand, chewed on a handful of dates and spat the seeds to the side. He scowled at the fire, as if it had wronged him personally.

"Insh Allah. He decided to let you live," Hassan said. "You should be grateful."

"Grateful?! Are you kidding? My camel, supplies, everything I had is gone!"

"You still have your life," Hassan pointed out.

"What kind of life is that?" asked Randy. "I can't even go back if I don't..." His voice trailed as he gazed into the fire again. Without his gear, he didn't have a hope or a prayer of returning to civilization.

"What have you been doing in the middle of the desert all by yourself?" Ophir asked. The other men, equally skeptical of Randy's presence, all scrutinized him with judgmental eyes. Few of them found his arrival to be mere coincidence. There had to be something sinister afoot. Or so they thought. The sad truth about it was that Randy was a hack treasure hunter on the search for his next big find. If he didn't strike it rich and return with something worthwhile, the debt collectors were going to be the least of his worries. He owed people money, and they were the kind of people no one wanted to remain indebted to for long.

"I am... an archaeologist," Randy finally offered, twisting the truth. "I look for ancient ruins, lost cities, civilizations, and forgotten relics. That kind of thing." And if he had anything to say about it, he'd make a fortune out in the desert once he turned up his next big discovery. It was all a matter of finding it first and getting people off of his case.

"Really? And what did you carry this for?" Ophir asked. He pulled Randy's revolver from beneath his robes. Vibrant orange light glinted off of the metal, reflecting the campfire nearby.

Randy's hands promptly flew for the gun. The Arabs drew their knives, and a dozen blades glinted beneath the moon's silver effulgence. Their convincing array of weaponry stilled his movement. He held up both hands, begging caution, and settled back again in his seat. It wouldn't help his situation at all if he was stabbed or shot full of holes by a group of cagey Arabs.

"I think you are not telling us the truth," Hassan said. "The only thing you can find here is..."

"A gate of Ganzir?" Idris spoke up drowsily. The young boy had slept on and off, drowsing until the raised voices of their interrogation awakened him. No one could sleep through that, especially while Randy ran his mouth.

"Hush, my son. Don't speak this name," Hassan said.

"You will bring bad luck on all of us," Ophir muttered. "Demons have big ears."

Randy visibly perked, sitting up from his slump. "Gate of Ganzir? What's that?"

"We do not play with dark forces. Tomorrow, we'll reach Yassa. You can go home from there," Hassan said.

After a disappointed sigh, Randy nodded his head and settled down for a night's rest. Tomorrow, he would be in

Yassa, and perhaps one step closer to his goal and to become a wealthy man.

***

By morning, the caravan had resumed traveling through the sea of rolling dunes. They didn't reach the Yassa Oasis until evening. Camp was set against the rocky outcroppings, and in the light of the descending sun, the caravan leader discussed Randy's fate.

Was he to be left and abandoned with no resources, or would they at the very least grant him a single camel? Hassan erred on the side of showing kindness, while the men in his service argued that Randy was the devil in sheep's clothing.

So of course, by morning Randy had split from the group to do the very thing that would prove them right.

Tinkling laughter, like silver bells, filled the early morning air. Hassan's four wives bathed in the oasis by the light of the rising sun, guarded by a large man by the name of Niyazi. The muscled eunuch held a machine gun and kept watch over the horizon.

Above them, Randy crouched amid some scraggly bushes and shamelessly peeked at the naked women. His mouth watered at the sight of them.

This is wrong. I shouldn't be watching them like this, but it's been so damn long since I saw a woman...

Ultimately, that niggling sense of guilt swayed Randy to turn away. While he hadn't set out with intent to become a peeping tom, their laughter and the sound of amusement had drawn him like a moth to the flame.

As he crawled backwards, the soil beneath his elbow shifted, loosened, and skittered into the pond below. One of the wives screamed and pointed. The others shrieked and dove deeper into the water, modestly covering their nubile bodies.

Oh, shit! Randy thought as he quickly scurried away. Niyazi's shrill war cry preceded the removal of a cell phone from his loose robe. Reinforcements were coming, and he didn't need binoculars to see them coming. Arab men abandoned their tasks, grabbed their weapons, and came rushing across the sands with their knives drawn.

In Randy's worst fantasies, he imagined them drawing and quartering him by camel then leaving his pieces to rot beneath the desert sun. With his stealth blown, Randy leapt up to his feet to flee for it on foot, to little avail, the sand shifted between the tumbling rocks and he toppled forward into the pool below.

The fight to return to the surface was difficult. He swam clumsily, panicked, and failed to find the bottom of the pond with his feet. Once he broke the surface, a bullet struck the rocks beside his head. More rounds disturbed the surface of the water and came dangerously close to gifting his body a few additional holes.

"Shit!" He went under again as the bullet storm created a shower of rocks. Their pebbles struck him in the head as he choked on water and went under again. Fortune must have been with him, since his terror sent him into a frantic up and down bobbing pattern that evaded the worst of their attack. Each time he came up for air, one of the Arabs swung a knife at him or shot another bullet.

Until Ophir struck him in the head with a rock. Sharp pain exploded from his temple and his cry resulted in a mouthful of water entering his throat. Randy's limp body sunk beneath the water as his head spun and stars danced in his vision.

The last thing he remembered as he hit the sandy bottom was the rumbling sound of dark laughter. The ground shifted beneath him, blackness edged into his fading vision, and then he fell back into oblivion.

***

Randy struck rocky ground with a hard smack. The crash was enough to send him into a coughing fit, expelling the water from his burning lungs. He gasped for breath and sank back into the darkness.

The slow drip of water roused him back to consciousness. Plink. Plink. Plink. He rolled to his side and blinked rapidly in an attempt to make out his dark surroundings. Dim light radiated from an unknown source but it allowed him to get his bearings.

He was on the edge of an underground lake in a rocky cavern. The single source of dripping water came from several feet above his head. He watched as a bead of moisture gathered itself on a jutting bit of rock until the weight of gravity drew it downwards.

Plink.

"Where the hell am I?"

Am I... am I... am I... His voice echoed back to him in the dark. The sound was unsettling and made the hairs at the back of his neck stand on end.

After a few minutes his eyes adjusted further to his foreboding surroundings. Secure in the knowledge that he was unhurt, Randy pulled himself up and set out. A rough staircase caught his eye across the cavern.

"Just my luck," he muttered. "I need a vacation. Treasure hunting is getting bad for my health."

The stairs appeared sturdy, cut into the very rock of the cavern, but they were steep. Randy tested the first slick step then took another one up. The tread on his boots was a saving grace on the wet stone.

"If I get out of here alive, I'll seriously consider a change of career."

The faint illumination coming from the opening above drew Randy onward with the promise of escape. Four steps up he hit a slimy patch and stumbled. Pain exploded in his kneecaps.

"God! I'm getting too old for this!"

Rather than an echo, a rumble answered his sharp cry. Dust rained down from overhead and a tremor shook the cavern around him, but that dimmed in comparison to the laughter that filled the air. The demonic sound froze the blood in Randy's veins. Terrified, he scrambled up the steps on all fours. The shaking didn't stop until he reached the top.

Randy sprawled on the floor and waited for his racing heart to slow. Lurching to his feet, he brushed off the dust from his clothes and ran a shaky hand through his hair. The dust settled and revealed the narrow, short corridor he occupied was a dead end. A crude gate blocked the passage. Further inspection revealed Arabic inscriptions carved into the stone archway.

"This place gives me the creeps," he muttered. Randy dug into his pocket and pulled out a slim, battered dictionary. Years of hard use had cracked the binding and dirtied the pages.

"Okay, let's see..." He rose to his tiptoes and tried to make the words out. "I wish there was more light in here."

"As you wish."

The deep voice came from nowhere. As if that weren't startling enough, the cave lit up with an eerie, orangish glow.

"Holy shit!" Randy's pulse spiked. "Whaaat waaas thaaat?"

Wild-eyed, he looked around the cavern for the voice. Gooseflesh prickled his arms when he spotted no one.

"You... are... standing..." His teeth chattered and his hands shook as he tried to translate. "Standing.. at... The Gate..." He wiped his sweaty brow and swore. "I wish this place came with a translating service."

The deep voice rumbled out a second time. "You are standing at the Gate of Ganzis. Beyond, lies the domain of the Archdemon Shabalis. Only the soulless can enter. Treasure of treasures..."

"Treasure?!" Randy exclaimed. His mind reeled with a thousand ways to spend a fortune. Women, alcohol, drugs - maybe not the drugs, as narcotics tended to deplete cash faster than cheap bottles of whiskey - and promises of fast cars quickly dashed any likelihood of him turning away.

"Don't interrupt!" the voice chastised him.

He frowned but ultimately decided to listen. Something in his heart told him that his luck was finally bound to change for the better. "Sorry. Go on, go on."

"Your heart is full of shadow. You are a soulless one. Enter and see for yourself."

"Sure. I could use a treasure." *Damn skippy I'm going to enter.*

Randy made his way through the entrance, and beyond the gate, he encountered a well lit, narrow passage. His greed drove him to explore the unknown and push forward even as the walls wavered. Their image shimmered and vanished into nothingness, taking with it the ground beneath his feet.

Randy plummeted into darkness.

Chapter 2

It didn't take long for Randy to become lost in a labyrinth of shady passages and dad-end caves. He wandered through the twisting catacombs for what seemed like hours before a light caught his eye. Cautious, wondering what might be found, Randy stepped into the roughhewn chamber.

A single pedestal rose up from the center of the room, directly beneath a shimmering globe of light. The luminous sphere hung suspended in the air with no visible source or holder.

Seven objects occupied the polished surface: A silver framed mirror, a brass lamp, an antique bottle, a ring with a large ruby, a crystal ball, a jar filled with a dark substance, and a short knife with a gem-encrusted handle. It sparkled in the light, casting radiant shimmers.

Driven by impulse, or perhaps his own stupidity, Randy reached for the ring and closed his fingers around the metal. It didn't go without a fight. The brilliant light flared, a miniature supernova that sizzled through his fingertips and seared into his skin.

"Shit!" Randy jerked his hand back and inspected the blistered stripe left behind. He swore again and glowered at the ring. "How the hell can I get it without burning myself..." Lacking gloves, and doubting that they'd be enough to withstand the heat, Randy removed his belt and made a loop. Using it as a tool, he snatched each of the objects from the pedestal. They clattered to the sandy ground where he quickly joined them to examine his ill-gotten goods.

"Where'd that ring go?" he muttered. Its primary jewel, the large ruby, winked in what remained of the light. He plucked it up from the ground and admired it. Greedy thoughts of how he'd spend his new fortune flickered through his thoughts. He'd be a wealthy man soon and able to get back on top of his business. Resume his explorations. And most importantly, he'd be able to buy a lot of alcohol and spend his time with numerous women. Randy grinned.

"The rest's just a pile of junk." He sorted through the relics and figured the knife would fetch a decent price. The bottle rolled across the floor and liquid sloshed within, drawing attention to Randy's parched throat. He pried the wax stopper free and gave the contents a wary sniff.

"Smell like wine. Pretty good, too."

Ignoring the thin stream of vapor rising from the bottle, Randy chugged the contents. Sweet wine danced over his tongue, oddly cool despite his muggy surroundings. He drained the bottle of every last drop, smacked his lips, and then wiped his wrist across his chin.

Stabbing pain lanced through his belly. Randy grabbed his middle and doubled over, his body convulsing. His heart pounded in his head and he lost all control of his limbs. Like a marionette on strings, he jerked around the room. Pain lanced through his gut and his stomach expanded.

Acid burned up his throat, followed by the contents of his stomach. Randy threw up all over himself and crumpled to the ground.

"So much for good wine... ugh." He couldn't recall the last time he'd felt so miserable.

A strange figure rose from the puddle of puke, expanding with each passing second until its masculine shape solidified completely. The stranger flicked little chunks of vomit from his exotic clothing, their design too old, too archaic to fit the current time period. "What a mess, but thank you. You've been most kind," the strange man said.

"Huh? Kind? Me? Neeeh. Who are you though, dude?"

"Just the same, thank you for freeing me. I'm Karim Khan, a genie at your service."

"A genie? Yeah, and I'm Alice in Wonderland."

"Who?"

"Never mind. I don't believe in fairy tales," Randy said.

"What makes you so sure?" Karim Khan asked. "I'm as real as you are. I'm here, aren't I?"

Randy touched Karim's rich, plum-colored garments. Embroidered threads of gold added intricate designs to the lush fabric. Jewels clinked and tinkled together with his movements. "This looks pretty expensive... Maybe you are a genie after all. You did come from a bottle. At my service, you said?"

"I am here to fulfill your every -- well almost every wish."

Randy squinted at the man in front of him. Karim didn't seem much older, in his early thirties perhaps. His well-groomed, jet black mustache and beard suited his brown features. A turban concealed his hair length, though for all Randy knew, the man could have been bald entirely.

"Great! Now I'm on to something. Let's start with…"

"Wait!" Karim cried. "First there is something I'd like you to do for me."

"I never do anything for anybody. That's my rule," Randy said.

Karim rolled his eyes. "I'm not alone. There are seven of us. Think of how much more seven genies could do for you. Money, riches, women, seven times more--"

I could be rich! Randy thought. He practically cackled as he rubbed his hands together and allowed the greed to overtake him. A storm of ideas flooded his brain with plans to purchase fast cars and women in lingerie. Well, fast cars anyway. He couldn't purchase the women, but he certainly planned to buy some of their time.

"Okay. What do I do?" Randy asked.

"Put that ring on and twist the ruby three times," Karim said.

Randy followed the instructions. A moment later, an elderly man in ornate robs appeared before them both.

"My cousin, Abdul Khandir," Karim introduced them.

Abdul dipped into a courteous bow.

"Good. Now take a crystal ball and rub it against your forehead," Karim instructed Randy.

"This really makes me feel stupid," Randy remarked. Despite his reservations, he plucked the crystal ball from the floor and rubbed the smooth crystal against his brow. In return for his cooperation, a middle-aged woman appeared next.

"My mother, Salima Khan. You look good, Mom."

Salima threw her arms around her son and kissed him.

"Very touching. Let's get on with it," Randy muttered. "I have somewhere to be after this." *Spending all of my riches and becoming the wealthiest man in the world.*

"Tap the lamp lightly," Karim said.

Randy gave it a rough thump.

"Gently!"

Randy tapped it again. As with the other objects, another genie appeared. This time it was a ten-year-old kid. The child wore extravagant clothing in rich colors and fine thread, but he lacked the turban donned by the older two male genies.

"A kid genie? This is going too far." Randy sighed. He didn't need a kid to do his bidding.

"You haven't seen anything yet, mister. My name is Aboo Khadir. What's yours?" the kid introduced himself.

"Don't get smart with me, you little brat. Just call me Randy."

"Yes, Master. Thank you for freeing me. I was getting bored."

Aboo looked around the cave and grimaced. "A nice mess Gengir Xul got us into."

"Don't mention his name," Karim said. "He may think it's an invitation."

A deep rumbling noise precedes the shudder of the underground chamber. The tremors nearly threw Randy off his feet.

"He has awakened," Abdul said. The genies wore matching expressions of terror on their faces. Something was definitely wrong.

"We have to get out of here, Master! Make a wish. Take us to your world," Karim said.

"Can I do that?" Randy asked. "Just make a wish and then we'll be somewhere else? Just like that?" The possibilities were endless. The very idea of going anywhere he wanted appealed to Randy's sense of adventure. Travel without plane rides, buses, trains, and better yet, the ability to travel without *paying*.

"Yes, but hurry. Gengir Xul will be here any minute, and you wouldn't like that," Salima warned him.

The genies gathered the objects that had trapped them along with the remaining relics.

"Where can we go?" Randy asked.

"Anywhere. Hurry!" Karim cried.

"Anywhere? How about... back home?"

"Just make a wish," Aboo encouraged.

"I wish to go to..."

A loud popping sound occurred before the world around Randy rotated and spun. It picked up speed, whirling exponentially faster like water spinning down an open drain until finally everything in Randy's vision blurred. When his surroundings snapped into focus again, he and the four genies materialized out of thin air, reappearing in the middle of Hollywood Boulevard. Motorists honked horns and shouted obscenities out of their open car windows. A hooker even waved at Randy and winked. She made a suggestive call and propositioned him from her street corner.

"Where do you think you are going, morons?" a cab driver yelled out of his window.

The confused genies didn't move until Randy pushed them toward the sidewalk.

"Take us to a more private place," Abdul suggested.

Karim offered another valuable piece of advice. "Be specific when you make a wish."

"Hurry! Somebody is coming," Aboo pointed out, jerking on Randy's sleeve with one hand and gesturing toward two cops with the other. The two stone-faced lawmen approached with haste.

Shit. I better think fast. "I'm starving. I want to eat something," Randy muttered.

"I'm hungry too," Aboo said. He jumped up and down like a typical child. "Where can we go?"

"I like Italian. Let's go to Pizza Hut. That okay with you?"

They vanished again.

***

Gengir Xul appeared in the middle of Hollywood Boulevard. He whirled on the spot, an ominous figure overshadowing the sunny afternoon. At least, he appeared ominous until a cab driver suffering road rage left his vehicle and kicked him out of the road.

"I've had enough of you crazies blocking the road! Get out of the way!" the driver screamed.

Gengir Xul pulled out a moon-shaped sword, curved as sharp as a sickle. Its radiant edge gleamed as he charged the cab driver, and yet he failed to meet his objective. Two police officers seized him. Once they disarmed Gengir Xul, they threw him to the pavement and searched him thoroughly before applying cuffs and placing him in their vehicle.

***

Multi-colored lights blinked from every corner of Pizza Hut. While Randy may have called it Italian, it was little more than a child's buffet wonderland pizza in different styles and flavor combinations.

Randy chowed into his buffalo chicken pizza without complaint while the genies made short work of their portions. And with each serving of pizza from the line, the streets beyond the window grew darker and darker. Shop lights came on, blazing strips of color against a brightly lit storefronts.

"This is great," Aboo cried! Apparently children loved pizza whether they were typical youngsters or magical, wish-granting beings.

Randy had to grin a little when the kid pulled another slice off of the platter.

"Not bad," Karim agreed. "We need to find a private place."

"Where do you live?" Salima asked Randy.

"I don't actually have a place. I just got kicked out of my apartment. My stuff is in storage."

"We have to find a safe place and set the wards before Gengir Xul finds us," Abdul said. When the older genie frowned, his forehead wrinkled like an old basset hound, practically drooping his large brows over his eyes.

Randy glanced over toward the approaching waitress. She held the bill in her hands, no doubt a fee totaling more than he had on him. Not that it was a difficult feat when he didn't have a single nickel to his name.

Karim rubbed his chin. "An abandoned house, perhaps. We must remain inconspicuous."

"Yeah, inconspicuous," Randy agreed. He sunk down into his seat when he spotted two cops stepping inside the diner. He held his menu up in an effort to hide his face. "I wish to find an empty house,"

"Say where," Aboo hissed.

"In Beverly Hills," Randy added on. "I wish to find an empty house in Beverly Hills."

They vanished from the table, leaving a startled waitress behind with the unpaid bill. In the span of three heartbeats, the group reappeared in a dark hallway. A quick look around revealed marble floors and a wide staircase leading up to the second level. A thick layer of dust and cobwebs in the corners ensured Randy the home hadn't seen occupants in a long time. Not even a cleaning crew.

"Perfect," Karim approved. "A few touches are needed here and there."

"Piece of cake!" Aboo chimed in. "I can do it myself."

Randy snorted. "Get out of here, kid. You still need somebody to wipe your nose."

"With your help, of course, my Master." Aboo put his hand over his heart and bowed.

"I don't help," Randy replied with a sneer. "That's my rule."

Randy almost felt a spark of regret when Salima drew Aboo into a protective embrace to soothe his injured feelings. She exchanged looks with the other genies then turned back to Randy. "Master, what he meant to say is that you have but to only make a wish and he does the rest."

The greedy gleam returned in Randy's eyes. "Well, in that case, I think it's okay. I wish for this place to look like a palace. Don't go light on it either, I want it to be amazing down to the last detail."

Everything changed in an instant. Dust vanished and the white floors sparkled beneath the light of a thousand oil lamps. The empty rooms filled with expensive oriental furniture, silk rugs, and embroidered tapestries. Precious jewels glittered from every corner. As a final touch, a fountain appeared in the middle of the hallway with clear-running water that trickled over a thick bed of glittering gold coins at the bottom. His own wishing fountain. Ha!

"Wow! This is a better deal than I thought." Randy grinned and couldn't believe his sheer luck. *I am gonna live like a king!*

Aboo beamed, proud of his handiwork. "I may be young, but I am a genie, remember? Do not underestimate us."

Randy rubbed his hands together and contemplated the many possibilities. "Oh wow. You mean you can give me money and power? Everything I want?"

Abdul nodded. "That is correct. With a few restrictions."

"So much for using you guys to help me with my job searching for old stuff. Why work when I can have it given to me. My treasure hunting days are over!" Randy clapped his hands and jumped around, darting from one room to the next. He turned sharply at the bottom of the stairs, his brow furrowed. "Hold on a sec. What restrictions?"

The genies all grouped together and faced him with solemn expressions.

"We cannot make anyone love you," Karim began.

Who needs love anyway? "Okay, I can live with that. What else?"

"We cannot enact your revenge," Abdul informed him. "Genie Code of Ethics #1."

"And be careful what you wish for. You will surely get it." Karim continued.

"No problem." Randy said. "How about if we start--"

Abdul held out a hand. "Wait!" he cried in warning. "There are still a few of us who are trapped. We need to free them."

"Fine," Randy said. "Okay, what do I do first?"

Karim plucked the gem-encrusted knife from the small table where the genie vessels were all neatly stored. They had been positioned in a neat circle. "Twist the sapphire at the tip of the handle," Karim said as he passed the weapon to Randy.

Randy balanced its cool weight on his palm and studied the ostentatious weapon. It was just his style, and the perfect tool he would have preferred to take on his treasure seeking adventures if it wasn't also a genie's home. Once he rotated the sapphire on the hilt, the next genie appeared in a flash. Randy nearly stumbled back and fell over his own feet to distance from the fearsome creature.

"Good to see you Tamujin," Abdul greeted him.

Over seven feet tall, with a grotesque face only a mother could love, the being known as Tamujin resembled a vicious bulldog. Wrinkled folds of skin overlapped caterpillar thick brows, and his thick, purple lips curled back from his pointed fangs. It was either a grin or a snarl, but Randy would have put money on it being the latter.

"I don't know about that..." Randy began. He fell back another step from the fearsome genie and craned his neck to look up at him.

"Tamujin is our cousin," Karim said. The genie's smile didn't reassure Randy much.

"Nice family," Randy said.

"Our common enemy," Karim said, in a bid to avoid using the Gengir Xul's name, "Transformed him many years ago before we became captive to our vessels."

Against his better judgment, Randy asked, "Why?" *It's not like I care about them or anything. I just need these guys to make me the wealthiest man in the world.* Despite his claims, he glanced at Tamujin's ugly face again and grimaced in sympathy.

"Tamujin was too powerful, too sure of himself, and too handsome. In his arrogance, he fell in love with the same girl loved by our enemy--"

"Broads always get you in trouble," Randy commented.

"I wouldn't mind some "trouble" every now and then," Karim muttered. "Sitting in a bottle for a thousand years is no fun."

Randy winced. He couldn't imagine enduring as long as Karim without the touch of a woman and her intimate company. And while it had been an irritating length of time since the last dalliance, he planned to fix that as soon as the rest of his affairs were in order. Like acquiring a new stretch limousine, or maybe a Ferrari.

"I agree," Randy said. "Twenty years would have been too long for me." *Let alone a thousand,* he thought. "Now why don't we go ahead and fix that by granting me my next wish. I have some ideas--"

The house rumbled and shook. Tremors spread throughout the opulent mansion until decorative objects on the shelves jiggled. A few rolled over the edge and fell to the floor, too delicate to withstand the distance.

"Gengir Xul!" Abdul cried in terror.

"Naaah," Randy said. He waved his hand in dismissal. "Just an earthquake. We're probably on a fault line here."

***

The filthy interior of a Los Angeles detention unit became Gengir Xul's temporary home. He sat alone on a bench, his clothing in a disarray, while blue sparks crackled along his body. His grim countenance intimidated his cellmates, who clustered in a corner of the chamber to grant him space.

Armed guards held watch outside of the secure metal bars.

"I've never seen anything like this before," the first officer said.

"Me either. Not in my nineteen years on the force. We better call and let someone know about this." He nodded his head toward the adjacent desk and an ordinary, nondescript black phone.

"You think so?"

They glanced from the phone back to the cell and regarded Gengir Xul with distrust. As if sensing their hesitation, he threw his arms to either side and roared. The resulting quake nearly knocked both officers from their feet.

"Yeah. Definitely. Call now!"

Chapter 3

The quake left the house in shambles. Broken glass and shattered ceramics littered the floor. Water from the fountain covered the marble floor in a slick puddle. It was a trip to the Emergency Room waiting to happen.

"Ugh. Looks like we need a maid," Randy complained. He kicked aside loose gemstones and a fallen silver chalice.

"Not so," Aboo told him. "Simply make a wish, Master."

"That's right, I have genies." Randy rubbed his hands together. "In that case, I wish for this place to look *grand*."

In a blink, the inside of the mansion transformed from a crummy mess into an opulent space. The chandelier sparkled, the floors were spotless, and more treasures had been added in addition to the fixed ones.

"Wow, this place looks even better. We could open a cleaning business. You guys would earn millions."

Abdul frowned and crossed his arms over his chest. "No time for jokes, Master. Set the rest of us free. We must set the wards before Gengir Xul finds us. He could find us at any moment."

"Hold up a minute, what is this all about?" Randy refused to budge. "Who is this Gengir Xul and why is he after you?"

"It is a long story," Karim replied.

Randy smirked. "I'm in no rush. You want me to free all of you, spill it."

"Once, long ago, we were a family of powerful magicians. We were human, like yourself.

***

The magicians labored over their most recent project. Abdul, Karim, and a third magician leaned forward over a table to examine a glowing creation in the middle of a magical circle. The chalk outline glittered over the wood surface, but at its center, precious stones shone with a surreal, prismatic light that cast beans of red, blue, green, pink, and yellow over their faces.

Magical paraphernalia surrounded them at every corner, ranging from fat candles imbued with alchemical additives to bones carved with special runes.

Through a mystical process requiring many moon cycles of tedious work, the two magicians had created Tanju, the jewel of all jewels, a superior stone of power with sway over the aspects of good and evil.

Abdul, one of the magicians, intended to use the Tanju to restore peace to the world, but darker forces had other plans in mind. Gengir Xul, a distant cousin, envied the power granted by Tanju. He coveted their gift for his own insidious desires until he made a pact with the Archdemon Shabalis. It was the ultimate betrayal.

In their own stinking cave, filled with the stench of demon's filth and despair, Gengir Xul and Shabalis performed a sinister ritual. They created a jewel of their own and heralded the beginning of the end for the magicians.

"I have a terrible feeling," Salima murmured suddenly. "Doom. Destruction. A terrible force approaches us."

"I feel nothing, Mother. Perhaps you are overworked and tired. There is nothing the matter, and at last, we will enjoy the fruits of our labors," Karim said.

Salima glanced away from the ancient map on the table to meet her son's eyes. Nearby, Aboo mixed cloudy liquid in an encrusted glass crucible. Despite his age, he had developed a profound talent for alchemy. His most recent creation could strip the poison from a dying man and restore him to vitality within minutes. He worked hard at his craft, aspiring to reach the same level of greatness as the rest of his family.

"That looks excellent, Aboo," Karim spoke up. "What will this do?"

"Aquatic breathing," the boy replied. "I want to be able to swim beneath the water without coming up for air. I think it will work."

"How will you test it without putting yourself in danger?" Salina asked. Her brow creased.

"I'll figure out something." Aboo smiled broadly, crinkling his eyes at the corner.

"What he means is that he will get into mischief of some kind to test it," Abdul muttered under his breath.

"I will no--"

A peal of cackling laughter interrupted their conversation. Salima trembled, a shudder running over her spine.

"There it is! Something is amiss as I forewarned," she said.

The air in the room wavered, shimmering like heat waves on an unforgiving summer day. As the room shuddered, besieged by a great quaking power, the magicians all stumbled as if struck by an unseen force. Moments later, they began to shrink until they were only inches tall, and at the completion of the dark act they were sucked toward the table and its objects: the lamp, the knife, crystal ball, and the ring. As Aboo was sucked shrieking in terror into his vessel, triumphant laughter filled the room.

***

"A powerful spell changed us into genies and trapped us for millennia," Tamujin concluded the story. Salima rubbed his arm in a gesture of support.

"Until you came and set us free," the older woman picked up the tale. "However, Gengir Xul received more than he bargained for. He became a demon."

"And now hordes of demons guard Tanju beyond the Gate of Ganzir. Deprived of light, the stone of power is dying."

Randy look unconvinced. He raised a brow and rubbed his jaw. "How can a stone die? It's not alive to begin with."

"This is a magical stone," Salima clarified.

Aboo nodded his agreement. "Unless somebody crosses the Gate of Ganzir and retrieves it in time, we will all be destroyed. Shabalis and his demons will rule..."

"End of the world," Karim whispered.

"Doom." Salima bowed her head.

"Hell will break loose." Aboo shuddered and Salima drew him close.

Randy lifted his hands, palms out, and shook his head. "Don't look at me. Remember my rules; I don't help."

"But..."

"Look, it's a nice fairy tale and all, but I'm not risking my neck for a bunch of... weirdos."

"We will give you anything you want," Karim offered. "Anything." Desperation edged his tone.

"You could help us as a friend," Aboo suggested.

"No way, kid."

Karim frowned. "A little gratitude would be in order."

"What part of 'no' don't you genies understand?"

Tamujin grunted. The large genie had held his silence save for a few words here and there. "He passed the Gate of Ganzir," the hulking man told the others in his deep voice. "That tells us something of his nature."

"Very well. In that case, first things first." Abdul offered the silver framed mirror to Randy. "Would you kindly hold this and wipe its surface clockwise thricely?"

Pushy jerks. I should show appreciation? They should show appreciation that I freed them. "Give me one good reason why I should do anything else. I have enough genies here to serve me without adding more of you to the mix."

Tamujin's lips curled back from his curved fangs as he released a primal roar. The snarling noise threatened to pop Randy's ears, the heat struck him in the face, and the immense treble generated by the ferocious sound shook their surroundings like a miniature earthquake. Regretting his tone, Randy shrank back from him a few steps.

"Reasoning is not my forte, I guess," Randy muttered.

Following the instructions, he wiped his hand across the mirror in a clockwise circle. Upon completion of the first pass a pretty face formed in the mirror. Her dark eyes reminded him of the tiger's eye gemstone and her lips formed a perfect bow. Her lovely features moved closer until they pressed against the glass, as if she were trying to push out.

Wow, she is hot! "Wait! Wait! I'm almost done." Randy hurried and finished the last two wipes across the reflective surface. A brilliant swirl of color rose up from the mirror like a miniature tornado. The maelstrom coalesced into a young woman. She hugged and kissed her fellow genies.

"Master, please, meet my sister Issa Khadir." Aboo made an exaggerated, gallant bow and swept his hand in a gesture toward the lovely woman.

"This is our new master?" Issa swept her gaze over Randy from head to toe. Her nose wrinkled with apparent distaste.

Salima stroked her hand over Issa's dark hair. "Be kind, child. We owe him our freedom."

"Some freedom." Issa's golden brown eyes flashed. "Now we will be his slaves."

Randy leered and roved his gaze over her curvaceous form. "Yeah, I like the sound of that."

"I bet you do," she snapped back.

"Enough of this." Karim looked between Randy and Issa, giving a stern look to the latter. "We have work to do."

"Here is the last of us. Please unscrew the top, Master." Abdul handed Randy the jar. Inside, a dark and viscous substance sloshed around. As troublesome as a pickle jar, Randy wrestled with the lid. After it finally popped off, a large blue and gold macaw materialized from the escaped vapor. The large parrot flapped its wings, soared around the room, and then landed on Aboo's shoulder.

"This is my brother, Badur," Aboo introduced. Of all the genies, he seemed the friendliest. "Ever since he was changed into a bird we call him Clip."

Randy jumped when the bird squawked and spoke. "Yak! I'm sick of it. Plum jam for a thousand years, every day," Clip complained. "I will never touch the stuff again."

Aboo tickled Clip's yellow breast feathers. "You loved plum jam. It was always your favorite."

"Not anymore. What took you all so long? You are all here having fun and I sit in a jar eating jam. It's not fair." Clip mantled his bright colored wings but Salima's soothing touch settled him back down.

"We did the best we could, Clip," Karim muttered.

"You could have done better, I' sure. But why am I not surprised."

"Great, a cranky bird genie is all I need." Randy ran his fingers through his hair and paced the hallway. All seven genies were freed but he wasn't sure if he was better off or not. Clip's raucous voice interrupted his thoughts, grating like nails on a chalkboard.

"I am always pushed back. Neglected. Now I am also insulted. What is this? Some kind of discrimination?"

"Would somebody shut him up before I shoot him? Is this bad karma or something?" Randy demanded.

The mansion rumbled and quaked, providing his answer. He turned and looked around the extravagant palace and drooped his shoulders in defeat.

***

"I've never seen anything like this before," the police detective said to his partner. The man within the cell, known as only Gengir Xul, was a mystery to the entire department. He had no history of incarceration or arrest, no social security number, and lacked even the most rudimentary forms of identification.

"Never met anybody without at least a credit card of some kind of him. Hell, he's a ghost," the other detective remarked. "No record, no warrants, no form of identification of any kind. Could be a terrorist from the Middle East."

"He's something. They said he used magic, Jones. Real freakin' magic. I don't know too many Taliban and members of ISIS able to use magic. This is something completely different."

Jones shook his head and stepped out of detention to return to his office. "Eh, I don't believe in magic. It's the intimidation factor probably. He scared the hell out of everybody and now they're all seeing things. Anyway, I'm going to go out to get a smoke. Think you can weather the storm in here and keep everybody from freaking out over one psycho?"

Davis followed behind him. "I'm telling you, there's something going on with this guy. When you weren't here, there were all kinds of sparks--"

"Get it on camera?"

"Well... no. He's just sitting there looking menacing while the others in the cell back away."

"Then it doesn't count," Jones said. "Davis, if you go telling the chief that this guy is shooting magic beams and electricity, he's going to send you in for a mental evaluation before the morning. Do you want that?"

"No," Davis said. He sighed.

"Great. So anyway, like I said, I'm going to get that smoke and you can hang out in here and babysit our psychopath. Let me know if he pulls a rabbit out of his hat next."

As Jones took the first step to leave, a quake rocked the entire city. Glass windows shattered and ceiling lights popped as frying computers burst into flame. The ceiling began to collapse as fleeing officers ran for cover to escape the chaos.

"Evacuate the cells!" Jones called to another officer.

"I can't! It's too dangerous!"

"Screw it, I'll do it!" Detective Jones took off at a run for the hallway only to see bolts of jagged electricity shooting from between the bars. He quickly turned and fled the Detention Unit instead.

He and Davis barely made it onto the street in time as the crumbling police department became a smoldering pile of ruin. A few police officers stood alongside the street with their hands on their pistols, while others secured a small handful of rescued prisoners liberated from their cells before the worst of the damage occurred. An unknown number remained inside the crumbling structure.

"Notify the fire department that we have a situation here. We're going to need backup and first responders to save the survivors," Jones barked into a police radio.

No sooner did they receive word that the fire department was en route, did a disheveled form stumble from the ruins of the detention center. The man known as Gengir Xul raised his brawny arms to either side of his body.

Davis drew his firearm and aimed. "Freeze! Put your arms behind your head and--"

Arcs of white lightning exploded from Gengir Xul's fingertips. One bolt lanced into Davis' chest and dropped him to the ground, smoking from the impact. His partner swore and aimed his handgun at Gengir to no avail. As parked vehicles burst into flame, the next bolt of electricity flew at Jones and he saw nothing more.

***

"Quickly, Karim, Gengir Xul is near!" Issa's eyes flared wide.

Karim patted himself down and searched through his various pockets. Randy counted at least six visible ones on the genie's pants alone and another two on his vest. He'd need a similar outfit the next time he went adventuring, if he ever went on another treasure hunt again. Who needed to work an honest day's living when a gang of genie servants waited at his beck and call?

"You didn't lose it, did you?" Aboo cried. On his shoulder Clip squawked and spread his azure wings.

"Rawk! Why don't I just go back to my jar and spare myself the trouble."

"Wait! I have it!"

Curious, Randy sidled closer to the frantic group. Karim held out a strange object comprised of thin golden wire shaped like a sphere roughly the size of a grapefruit.

How the hell did he not feel that in his pockets? Then again, how did it even fit in there? The answer was both simple and impossible - genie magic.

Karim and the others all placed their hands over the metallic ball. All seven of them wore equally grave expressions. "Master, place your hands over the Ward and say, 'I wish to activate.'"

"What is this thing?" Randy leaned over but made no move to touch it. *It looks like a Christmas ornament.*

Another tremor shook the mansion and an ominous roar rumbled overhead, deeper than thunder. Issa flinched, Aboo whimpered, and the others looked around with varying degrees of fear. Except for Tamujin. The large man leaned over Randy and bared his fangs.

"Do it!" Tamujin roared. Randy leapt back, startled more by the genie than the quaking house.

"All right! Okay! Geez!" Trembling, Randy moved back over and placed his hands with the others over the strange object. "I wish to, uh, activate."

Brilliant blue light exploded outwards, blinding in its intensity. Randy ducked back, reminded of the scalding light from the caverns, but the glow passed by him without harm.

"What *is* that?"

"It is the Ward," Karim explained. He took the glimmering sphere and set it at the pinnacle of the fountain. "A dome of magic surrounds this property now and will hide us from Gengir Xul."

"You're sure."

"Most certain."

Randy peered out the window into the darkened lawn. "I'll take your word for it," he said to the genies.

By morning, the family of genies was settled and comfortable in their new home. Randy woke to a veritable feast of breakfast delights, everything fit for a sultan. He gobbled up his meal like a starving man seeing food for the first time and washed it all down with orange juice mixed with vodka.

"So, time to make this all legit. There's a For Sale sign out in the front so we need to deal with that," Randy began once he was stuffed to the brim. "Don't want realtors dropping by unexpectedly." *Or cops.*

He pulled out his phone and dialed the number on the outdoor sign. Five rings later a cheery voice picked up on the other end of the line.

"T.J. Realty Specialists, this is Kimberly. How may I help you today?"

She sounds hot. Randy grinned into the phone. "Yeah, hi. I'm interested in one of your listings. 1122 Bel Air Vista Drive."

"A fine property, sir," the realtor replied. A note of excitement crept into her voice. "I can show you the property today at three if you like, Mister..."

"I've already seen it," Randy pushed on, passing over her fishing request for his name. "I want to buy it."

Kimberly's breath hitched audibly. "Of course, sir. In that case I can print out some paperwork for you to come in and look over at my office. Would four work for you?"

"Four is fine, but I'd rather you came to the property with everything," Randy told her.

"Er... All right, I can certainly arrange to meet you at the property. I'll be there at four o'clock sharp."

"See you then, Kimberly." Randy disconnected the call and tossed the cellphone to the side. "So she'll be here later today. This had better work."

"Of course it will work," Karim assured him. "Simply tell us how much you will need for the purchase and we will see it done."

Aboo joined them on the couch with a platter covered in honey soaked pastries and plump dates. Clip snatched up treats from his perch and the youngest genie's shoulder.

"What are you watching?" Aboo asked.

A live broadcast from the L.A Detention Unit dominated the news. Firemen, paramedics, and police officers moved around in the background while the reporter, a professionally dressed Asian woman, faced the camera.

"Last night the Detention Unit was the site of a terrorist attack," the woman informed the viewers. "Numerous explosions devastated the left wing of the building, which you can see behind me. Five guards and seven inmates were killed during the attack."

A good-looking man in his early thirties stepped into view, joining the reporter. She welcomed him with a small smile and a shake of her hand. Jaw clenched, Randy stared hard at the television screen.

"Inspector Rick Connor, you've been put in charge of the investigation. What can you tell us about this fatal incident? Are there any clues leading to the party responsible?"

"We are still searching the ground, but we have the situation under control. We will release information to the public after we have made a full evaluation of the incident," Inspector Connor relayed, cordial and to the point.

"I hate him," Randy spat. He tossed his cake at the screen.

Aboo jumped in his seat. "What's the matter, Master? Hate who?"

"*Him.*"

Aboo and Karim exchanged uncertain looks. "The man on the news? Why?"

"I spent seven years in the can because of that guy, that's why." Randy jabbed his finger toward the screen. "Seven years!"

Clip screeched and flapped his wings in agitation. "Well welcome to the club. You sure you're not one of us? Was there anything to eat in there?"

"In *prison*, stupid," Randy corrected him.

Clip shot a dirty look to Randy. "Don't call me stupid," he fussed back at his human master.

The very sight of the inspector on the television boiled Randy's blood and made him see red. He took a few deep breaths and wished for a shot of scotch to soothe his addled nerves. Karim handed it to him obediently.

"What were you in prison for?" Karim asked.

"Just trying to make a living," he replied. "Rick was investigating the case. He si good. He's always the best of everything, anyway, and I was the black sheep of the family." Despite the passage of years, little had alleviated Randy's heartache and the sense of betrayal coloring his outlook toward his brother.

"Family?" Aboo asked.

"He's my brother, and I hate him."

"On that note, I think we'll go put ourselves to good use," Abdul muttered.

While Randy sulked and brooded on the couch, his efficient team of genies converted an upstairs bedroom into an elaborate alchemy lab. By the time Randy traveled to the upper level for a look, they had summoned most of their belongings, set up flasks and beakers, and crafted an assortment of occult baubles. Something sparkled from the corner of his eye, a flask with iridescent, ever-moving sparkles twinkled in the dim light. A bubbling beaker with some foul smelling concoction glowed above a low flame.

Aboo worked over the table with a tiny knife, slicing a plant intended for a herbal concoction. He scooped the diced stems into a small cauldron and stirred its contents with a fixed expression of consternation on his youthful face.

At another table, Abdul and Tamujin leaned above a black mirror. Randy approached to have a look over their shoulders. A glance at the dark surface revealed Gengir Xul crossing the street as a truck came barreling toward him at high speed. The driver honked the horn to no avail -- Gengir braced himself and turned to face his enemy, prepared for a fight. The truck flattened him and continued, undeterred by the human speed bump.

"Oh shit! Is he dead? Is it done that easily?" Randy asked.

"Doubtful," Tamujin said. His dark lips curled back from his fanged teeth.

"What? A truck just hit him! It was going full speed, there's no way he can be alive."

"Watch and learn, Master. Gengir Xul is far from human, and it will take more than one of your human contraptions to defeat him," Abdul informed Randy.

The trio stared at the mirror, but Randy's hopes were dashed when Gengir stirred and picked himself off the asphalt. The sorcerer limped toward the side of the road.

"Strange animals in this place," Gengir Xul muttered. He fell into a gutter to pass out into a deep slumber.

Abdul and Tamujin looked at each other and smiled. Gengir Xul wasn't dead, but for a while he would be slowed down and unable to seek them. That was good enough for now.

Chapter 4

The real estate agent, Kimberly, arrived sometime after noon. With her briefcase in hand, she unlocked the door with her key just as Randy dragged it open and gazed out at her. Startled, she jerked back and practically tumbled off of the extravagant stoop thanks to her four inch pumps. Randy reached out and caught her around the waist with one arm, not entirely for unselfish reasons. She was a hot little fox with a pretty face.

"Thanks for coming on short notice like this, Ms. Bryan."

"Thank you," she said after she caught her breath.

Randy released her from the partial embrace and invited her inside with a sweep of one arm. Her eyes grew larger and rounder with each passing second.

"This place looks better than I thought it did."

"I made a few improvements," Randy said.

"Er... how did you get a key to the home, Mr. Connor?" Kimberly asked.

The truth wasn't an option so Randy spun a little white lie and hoped that she bought it. He didn't know much about buying fancy homes. "The door was open. Come on. Let's sign the papers and get it over with."

He led the way through the house and into the main living room where Abdul and Karim cheerfully watched television. The family of genies wisely traded their Arabian garb for Western wear to blend into the community. They'd draw less questions if they didn't look like a team of cosplayers. Both genies rose from their seat on the when Kimberly entered the room.

"These are my business associations." To be downright technical it wasn't a lie. The genies were his business partners in a way. He kept them free from their vessels and in exchange, they worked for him. It was a fair trade in Randy's mind and mutually beneficial. He gave a passing wave toward the two genies but didn't bother with names.

"Pleased to meet you," Kimberly greeted in a polite voice. Her gaze darted around the richly appointed room.

"The pleasure is ours." Karim bowed. "May we offer you refreshments? Coffee? Tea?"

"No, thank you. I think we should get down to business." She perched on the edge of the couch cushion and opened her briefcase. "If you don't mind me asking, are you related to Inspector Rick Connor?"

Randy grit his teeth but forced himself to smile. "We're brothers."

"Oh! Okay. Well, I'll go over the terms with you, Mr. Connor. First, we'll-- oh!"

Clip glided over and landed on the realtor's shoulder, startling her enough to drop her pen. He whistled and rubbed his beak against her freckled cheek.

"Pretty lady," the parrot squawked.

"It's okay. He is only being friendly, I promise," Karim assured her.

Randy rolled his eyes. He didn't appreciate the little buzzard muscling in on his territory. As far as he was concerned, he'd called dibs on any opportunities with the sexy real estate agent.

"Right... okay... So, let's go over the terms," Kimberly said.

"Never mind the terms," Randy cut in. He shooed Clip off Kimberly's shoulder. "I'm hoping you know your job, so tell me. What's the price?"

Kimberly shifted in her seat and straightened out the paperwork pile. "The asking price was dropped about a month ago and is below the market value."

"I'm not here to haggle with you, Kimberly. May I call you Kimberly? Just name the price."

"Two and a half million dollars," she answered.

Holy crap. "Sounds fair. Give me a moment with my associates."

Randy gestured at Karim and Abdul then moved off across the room. The moment they were out of earshot he leaned in close.

"It's a damn rip-off," he hissed at the two genies. "I've never seen that much money in my life and this house was crap when we got here. Why can't we just make the house ours? Skip the paperwork."

Abdul shook his head. "We cannot change a thing's ownership."

"Another one of your dumb rules?" Randy snorted. "Just as well, things need to look official in this day and age."

"Okay, make a wish. How do you want it? Gold, diamonds, currency?"

"I wish for two and a half million dollars in thousand dollar bills." The kind of high denomination bills only the banks carried. Randy never saw one in person, but he eagerly rubbed his palms together and waited for the genies to grant his most recent desire.

The result was prompt, an open briefcase with neat piles of money appearing within seconds. Initially, Randy's jaw hung open and he stared in disbelief, still struggling to comprehend that magic, genies, and unlimited wishes were real. He picked up a stack of bills and thumbed through it, just to feel the crisp green notes beneath his skin. He'd never held so much money before. Once he returned the money to the briefcase, he snapped it shut and they rejoined Kimberly.

"Here's the money. Where do I sign?"

Amusement lit across the woman's features. She chuckled and glanced between him and the solemn-faced men in their company. "Mr. Connor, certainly you don't keep millions of dollars with you," she replied. "A check will be sufficient."

Randy set the case across his lap and flipped up the lid. She stared at him in disbelief. Before she could open her mouth, Tamujin entered the room. While he was no doubt attempting to smile, his hideous features contorted into a snarling grimace instead. His black lips tugged back from his sharp teeth, which glistened in the light. The sunlight's reflection against his eyes made them cast an unnatural red gleam, and for those brief moments, he looked like a demon himself.

"Uh... uh..." Kimberly began, paralyzed with fear. The motionless real estate agent stared.

"It's all right," Clip said. He rubbed his beak against her shoulder, a reassuring gesture that was all too human and intelligent for a parrot. "He's not as bad as he seems."

Kimberly's muscled tensed and drew tight, revealing her intentions to make a break for it. Between Clip's eery intelligence, Randy's suspicious briefcase of loot, and Tamujin's terrifying features, it became apparent Randy's chances of a personal conversation were shot.

"I... I have to go," Kimberly said. Her eyes flicked from the bird to Tamujin. Shaking, she got to her feet, barely able to balance on her weak legs.

"But what about the signatures?" Randy asked.

She scooped the contract into her briefcase, grabbed the money, and ran for the door. "Your contract will be in the mail."

The realtor didn't look back. She made her quick escape to safety, and seconds later, squealing tires announced her departure.

Randy sighed. So much for that.

MARIA COWEN

Chapter 5

A black dressed figure crept through the darkened room. Glittering jeweled bracelets and rings sat in display behind glass cabinets. The masked thief stuffed the expensive baubles in a sack, grinning all the while over each trinket. He wasn't selective. Each and every piece made its way into his possession. They'd sell for big money, and he already had a buyer set up, eager to acquire his haul.

The silence was shattered when the door burst open. Rick Connor led a swarm of armed officers into the store. Two on his heels were dressed as bums on the street, a pair of lowlifes he hadn't even paid attention to when he broke into the jewelry store. They were just out there milling by the street corner, one seated down with his half empty liquor bottle. It never occurred to him that he was playing into a sting arranged by the local law enforcement. Not once, did he even consider the awful consequences if someone knew and expected him to rob the store.

The officers trained their firearms on the masked thief, but the one in the lead appeared most prepared to shoot. He had a direct shot for the burglar and the rear door of the shop was too great a distance to make a run for it.

"Freeze! Get down on the ground! Hands behind your head!"

Without an alternative that didn't involve getting a bullet punched through his chest, the thief lowered to his knees. His obedience didn't earn him leniency. They disarmed him and threw the kneeling burglar to the ground, put their knees in his back, and secured him. A gun pressed to his temple.

They were going to kill him right there. LAPD didn't intend to take him in alive, they were going to kill him and claim he'd fought. A gruesome scenario flashed through the burglar's mind.

"About time we got this guy," one cop muttered. "Just make one move, creep. One move."

Despite the thief's cooperation, the body atop him didn't budge. The heavier cop had enough bulk to compress the criminal's lungs. Fear of suffocating made him squirm and struggle beneath the law enforcement officials, an act they took as refusal to obey. They struck him. A fist hit his kidneys, another struck him in the ribs, in the back. They boxed him in the head.

"Stop resisting!"

"I'm not resisting!" he screamed back at them. The world around him swam out of focus, and after ten long, excruciating seconds, the beating ended with him panting on the floor.

"That's enough. He's not resisting. He's already cuffed, so get off of him," Connor ordered. The order came a little too late. Liquid heat soaked the burglar's skimask, blood trickling from a head wound. Someone had pistol whipped him. "You have the right to remain silent. Anything say can and will be used against you in a court of law. You have the right to an attorney. If you cannot afford an attorney, one will be appointed to you."

"Let's see who we have, sir," another cop said.

Rick Connor ripped the skin mask away. He gasped at the sight of his own brother's face. "It's you again!"

The beating had made Randy delirious with pain. He spit blood out of his mouth before he replied. "Who did you expect? Roger Rabbit?"

"Damn it, Randy. Mom was right. You'll never learn."

They hauled Randy to his feet and jerked him out of the shop to the police car waiting outside.

Randy thrashed in his sleep and woke with a strangled yell. Sweat beaded his brow and soaked his shirt. He hadn't had that particular dream in months.

It's all Rick's fault. Everything since that night, it's his fault.

Anger boiled in his gut and drove him from the rumpled bed. He threw on some jeans and then padded barefoot out into the hallway. Greyish light from the pre-dawn sky filtered through the tinted windows.

I'll make him pay, Randy thought with vicious glee. *This time I'm the one with the power.*

He reached a door down the hall that the genies had claimed for their own use. He knocked, loud, and entered without waiting for an invitation. "Good, you're awake."

Abdul, Karim, Tamujin, and Salima were gathered around a small table covered with arcane trinkets and a city map. Randy had given up trying to decipher whatever strange rituals the family meddled around with in their own time.

"I have a wish," he announced.

"Could it wait?" Karim asked. "We are in the middle of something really important."

"No, it can't," Randy snapped back. "I wish to punish my brother, Rick Connor. I wish him beat and miserable. Hell, I wish him dead."

The genies all stared at him. Abdul was the one who stepped forward and shook his head. "We cannot fulfill such a wish, my son."

"Why the hell not? And I'm your master, not your son. It's your *job* to fulfill my every wish."

Salima joined Abdul. "Not this one, Master. We cannot harm anyone."

"Again I ask, why the hell not?" Randy's fists clenched at his side.

"Ethics. Universal Genie Law number one, section eight states that no intentional harm by means of revenge is allowed." Karim told him. "We tried to tell you this before."

A mottled red flush heated Randy's entire face and the vein in his temple throbbed. "I won't take no for an answer! I can't sleep. I can't eat. I want Rick to suffer!"

"Oh, you can eat." Clip soared down from his perch on a tall bookshelf and settled on the edge of the table. The parrot gobbled up the last date on a nearby platter.

"Shut up, Polly." *Stupid bird brained genie.*

Clip flapped his bright feathered wings. "My name's not Polly!"

Abdul raised his hands in a placating gesture. "Master, please, calm down."

Randy ignored him and shot a dirty look at Clip. "What am I doing here, arguing with a stupid bird."

"Don't call me stupid!"

"You genies are going to to grant my wish like you're supposed to."

Tamujin stepped forward fangs bared. "We said no," the large genie roared. "Now get out of our room."

"This isn't over." Rage made his entire body feel like a live wire. Randy stormed from the room and headed downstairs. *Tell me they can't grant my wish will they,* he fumed in silence. *I'll show them. Somehow I'll make them see who's boss.*

He threw himself down on the couch and scooped up the remote, jabbing his thumb down on the power button. An early morning infomercial for the 900 Psychic Friends Network filled the screen, promising answers to all your most pressing questions regarding the future.

Golden coins jangled from around the neck of the woman onscreen and a colorful scarf covered her hair. The clashing colors reminded Randy of a clown at the circus, too bright and gaudy to be taken seriously. She peered into a crystal ball and asked the current caller about what she wanted to know.

"I just really wish I could find a good guy," the unseen caller said. "You know? So can you tell me if there's a man in my near future who won't be a loser?"

It was like a lightbulb went off over his head. Randy sat up as the first stirrings of an idea tiptoed through his mind.

This'll be perfect, he thought with a wicked smile. *Just perfect.*

Chapter 6

Kimberly Bryan practically collapsed against the console of her exercise bike. The Lifecycle was a spur of the moment purchase months ago that yielded few results. She wanted to fit into her pre-pregnancy bikini one day, but her hopes were dashed by the half a birthday cake she helped her son consume over the weekend.

"This movie is great!" Luke exclaimed from the couch. Her son and Floppy the labrador sprawled on the sofa. The pup rested his face on his boy's lap, whining on occasion until Luke scratched him behind the ears.

"Did you finish your homework, Luke?" The exhausted woman wiped sweat from her brow and took a long swig of water from the Aquafina in the cup holder.

"Almost, Mom." Luke focused on the airing of Streetfighter on the television. Jean-Claude Van Damme kicked a man across the screen, utilizing his trademark roundhouse kick.

"Go to your room and finish it *now*."

Luke and Floppy gazed at her in a silent plea. He practically begged with his eyes, reminding her of his father. His good for nothing father who left her with all of the responsibility. Kimberly sighed and shook her head. The sad face didn't work on her anymore, years of motherhood building her immunity to cute smiles and weepy expressions.

"But, Mom, I want to watch Jean-Claude Van Damme."

"After your homework," she insisted.

She plucked the remote from the cup holder and flipped channels. An unfamiliar infomercial played on one of her favorite stations, advertising 900 Genie Network.

"That's a new one," she muttered. She returned to her fast pedaling on the workout bike, determined to shed another five pounds from her thighs before the height of the summer beach season. An infomercial was just the ticket to boring her son into his room to complete his studies. She hoped it would motivate him to earning his time with Jean-Claude van Damme.

"Wait... I know that man."

In the studio, her most recent real estate client sat across a table from a gorgeous television hostess. Her fake enthusiasm grated on Kimberly's nerves. The hostess must have failed to become a news anchorwoman at some point in her life.

"What inspired you, Mr. Connor, to open this wonderful service to the public."

The hostess flashed Randy a pretty smile, frozen beneath a heavy layer of cosmetic foundation and Botox. Plastic surgery reduced her features to a caricaturization of a news anchor. Too pretty, too perfect, from her narrow nose chiseled by a doctor's scalpel to her high, permanently arched brows.

"Whoever did your work needs to give you back the money," Kimberly huffed. She leaned forward against the handlebars for a break.

"I was inspired by my family," Randy said.

"How did you recruit genies to work for your network?"

"I went all the way to the Middle East to find the creme of the creme, the best of the best."

The hostess turned from Randy to the camera. "Mr. Connor and his genies brought 900 services to a new level. You can be sure, you'll be talking to one of the best."

The 1-900 number flashed at the bottom of the screen in bold red print, commanding the viewer to call right away.

"My genies are very happy to be able to fulfill my clients' every wish. They take great pride in their work."

"I've heard that 900 Genie Network receives thousands of phone calls a day. It has brought amazing changes in many people's lives."

The scene faded from the commercial studio to a quaint living room in a suburban house. An attractive, middle-aged woman, sat beside a telephone bordered by grandmotherly knick knacks."

A split screen revealed the smiling hostess' to be beaming at the camera. "Linda Madeiros from Springfield, Ohio struggled with her weight problems since childhood."

During the introduction, a photo montage revealed pictures of Linda as a chubby child, an overweight teen, and finally an obese adult barely able to fit into a chair.

"I was three hundred and sixty pounds overweight with serious heart problems. My eating disorder was so bad that the doctor's didn't give me much hope. They wanted to put staples into my stomach so that I couldn't eat, and said that if I didn't make a lifestyle change, I wouldn't see another year," another voice said, presumably Linda. The voice over continued without revealing the new Linda. "I saw the 900 Genie program and called immediately."

Linda came into view in a chair. She was smaller than any of her photographs with a slender shape fit into a sleek, tight fitting black dress. After spinning in place, she spread her arms out at her sides. "Look at me now. I have a new life and it's all thanks to Mr. Connor and his 900 Genie program. Call him today!"

The screen faded again to a farm where an elderly couple smiled from beneath their stetsons. Behind them, the camera videoed cattle grazing in the pastures beside a single story, ranch-style home. A stereotypical red barn was in the distance.

"Betsy and Andy Eddings were losing their farm due to unpaid taxes. Eviction notices left them with no place to go."

Andy put his arm around Betsy's shoulders and held her close.

"We didn't know what to do. My family owned the farm for three generations," Betsy said.

"I had nightmares about my family living on the street. There was no help from anywhere. Our son, his wife, and his grandkids live here with us to help run the farm. This isn't only our home, it's our family business and our way of life."

A swarm of children ran across the grass. Two of them pulled kites across the blue skies. A dog barked and gaze chase after a ball. The scene was a perfect depiction of everyday family life.

"Then we saw your program. We're just lucky we dialed that number. We found oil on our farm, paid our debts, and we are rich. We can help to put our grandchildren through college now. Our entire family is overjoyed, and we have 900 Genie to thank for giving us a new chance at life."

The scene faded from the happy extended family to a gym. Men and women pumped iron in the background behind a muscular man with a handsome smile. His brilliant smile featured two rows of perfect, tidy white teeth suitable for a Colgate commercial. Athletic young women hung on to him from both sides.

"Harold Nichols was in his seventies," the hostess announced.

The scene faded to reveal a twisted old man with a spine bent like a question mark. He barely remained standing with the help of a cane. As the hostess spoke, his toothless smile remained frozen on the screen in a still image.

"He wished to be young again. How does it feel, Mr. Nichols, to regain your youth?"

"It feels great. Calling your Master Line was the best move I have ever made. I've been lonely ever since my Meredith died ten years ago of breast cancer, and while I couldn't bring her back with me, I have a fresh start at finding another wife."

The girls alongside him giggle and one pats his large bicep.

A gradual transition faded from the gym back to the interview screen where Randy stood next to the sexy hostess. They both smiled at the screen.

"Get some help. Call us 24 hours a day. Our genies are not just mere genies; they are Master Genies. They'll fulfill your every wish and leave you satisfied."

"Don't delay," the hostess said. "Call now."

"Select between 900 Master Genie, and 900 Master Junior Hotline. We even provide the popular 900 Master Pet Line for our little friends."

"All it takes is a telephone and an open mind."

Kimberly sat back on the machine and stared at her television. A genie's wish had to be better than all of the hard work and few results.

"Wow!"

"Wow!" Luke exclaimed from the door.

Floppy, their golden retriever, howled loudly.

"Didn't I tell you to go to your room, Luke?"

Her sulking son dragged from the room, taking the dog with him. The moment he was gone, Kimberly hurried for the phone.

Am I really about to do this? She stared down at the number pad. *Yes. yes I am.*

She punched in the number and counted down the rings. After three, the line picked up.

"Hello, I'm Kimberly," she said in a rush.

"My name is Tamujin. What can I do for you?"

Wow, he has a deep voice. "Is this for real? Are you really a genie?"

"I may not lie. I am what I claim to be," he replied. "What is it you wish for, Kimberly?"

"I want to be beautiful. Taller, like 5'9" or so, she said while she cast a quick look into her hallway mirror. "I want my hair to be long and lush, and blonder than it is now. And I want sky blue eyes, bigger boobs, and flawless skin without all these freckles. I want to be the perfect size. Oh, and I want to be a success."

"Sorry, Kimberly, but we have a strict one wish limit per call. Which will it be - beauty of success?"

"Beauty." She didn't have to think about it for more than a nanosecond and blurted out her reply right away. "I want to look great."

"As you desire," Tamujin replied. "I grant you your wish."

Within the next instant, Kimberly underwent a painless transformation. Her height bumped up a couple of inches, her body slimmed through her middle and curved out at her breasts and hips, and her hair thickened. She spun around in front of the mirror in an attempt to look over every inch, absolutely awestruck.

"Oh my god it happened. You really did it," she gushed over the phone. "Thank you! Thank you so much!"

"Thank you for calling the 900 Master Line," Tamujin replied. The line clicked and disconnected but Kimberly didn't care. She squealed with glee and spun around again.

"My homework is done," Luke called out down the hall. "You wanna check-- mom?"

Luke skidded to a halt and gaped at his mother. Floppy wormed between his legs and approached with cautious sniffs.

"Isn't this wonderful, Luke? It's my new look."

"Oh wow, mom, you look great. Different, though." He reached for the phone n her hand. "Can I call? I want to be a Power Ninja."

"Absolutely not. It's bedtime for you, young man. Besides, I hate that show."

"But mom," he whined.

"No buts, kiddo. Now get to bed."

***

Luke peeked out his bedroom door into the darkened hallway and waited. He strained his ears until he picked out the soft sound of his mother's snores, then he tiptoed out to the living room. Stealthy as a mouse, he picked up the phone and dialed the 900 Master Junior Hotline.

"Thank you for calling 900 Junior Genie Hotline. My name is Aboo."

"Hi, Aboo, my name is Luke," he whispered into the receiver.

"Hello, Luke. It is Luke, right? Can you speak a little louder? I can barely hear you."

"Yeah, that's my name."

"What wish might I grant for you tonight, Luke?" Aboo asked over the phone.

"Can you make me a Power Ninja?"

"A power who?" Aboo's confused voice made Luke giggle.

"A Power Ninja," he repeated. "You know, like the show? The orange guy is my favorite."

"You have to phrase it as a wish," Aboo told him.

"Oh. Okay." Luke took a deep breath, excited and nervous all at once. "I wish to be a Power Ninja."

"Coming up!"

Chapter 7

The city of Los Angeles never slept. The phones rang throughout the night, a never ending supply of frivolous wishes and requests for cosmetic surgery. Within the mansion walls, the exhausted genies manned the phone lines and approached their wit's end.

"I wish to have my boyfriend back."

"I wish to have a million dollars."

"I wish to flatten my tummy."

"I wish for a date with Fabio."

"I wish my dog would stop peeing on my carpet."

"I wish to have the biggest bone in the world."

"I wish to have a Lamborghini."

"I wish to be a sex god."

I wish... I wish... I wish...

"I have never heard so many stupid wishes in all my life." Aboo flopped down on the sofa in the living room and pulled a pillow down over his face. Issa joined him, curling up at the younger genies feet. Their spirits were so low that when Clip roosted on the armrest and ignored the tray of sweets laid out on the table. He had no appetite, even for his favorite candies.

The phone rang and all three genies shared the same look of disgust. None of them moved to answer.

"He can't do this to us," Issa seethed.

"But he is our master," Aboo reminded her without enthusiasm.

"Bah! I would rather return to my mirror."

Clip nodded his feathered head in agreement. "It's true. I'm so down I have no appetite. At least in my jar no one forced me to work this way."

"We're not even getting paid," Issa added.

Aboo sighed. "We cannot go back. He locked our vessels in a safe deposit box at the bank. To keep the safe, he said."

"I think I'm going to be sick," Clip cried. Aboo stroked his fingers down the parrot's back.

"I know, Clip, I know. But what can we do?" the youngest genie asked.

Issa jumped to her feet and tossed her dark hair over her shoulder. "I refuse to be his slave. I'm going out."

"But how?" Clip asked.

"We're genies," Issa said. "We have magic. Let's *use* it."

"I'm coming with you, Issa. Besides, I have an idea." Aboo hopped up with renewed vigor and darted across the room. He disappeared out into the hallway only to return a brief moment later with a rolled rug in his arms. Issa clapped her hands then hurried over to help him roll it out on the floor.

"Don't forget me!" Clip glided over. He settled on Aboo's shoulder.

The three genie uttered a quiet incantation in unison, allowing their magic to flow out into the rug. Light shimmered and energy twined through every fiber until the entire carpet glowed with a faint luminescence.

Slowly, the rug rose into the air, higher and higher. Aboo whooped in excitement and guided their ticket to freedom toward the open window.

The bright lights of Los Angeles lit up the sky and spread out before them like a stretch of multicolored stars. They flew their magic carpet high up in the sky, marveling in the view.

"Have you ever seen a city so big? So mighty?" Aboo asked the others.

"It outshines all the jewels that oaf has us conjuring for him," Issa replied. Clip cackled in agreement.

"And the ocean," Aboo continued in awe. "Look how wide it is, Issa! After living so many years in the desert I never expected to see such a sight."

"What's that?" Clip chimed in. "A metal bird?"

A helicopter appeared in the distance and without further warning, veered toward the kids on their flying carpet. Someone had discovered them. The big aircraft advanced on their magic object, and through the semi-translucent pane of glass at the front, they saw two open-mouthed men staring at them.

"Oh no!" Issa cried as an air current nearly swept her from the carpet. Clip clung with his claws, desperate to remain in place, but Aboo and Issa struggled to maintain a grip on the gold-threaded tassels.

The noisy rotor hurt their ears and whipped them with turbulent force. They spun and flipped out of control as each powerful whoop-whoop-whoop of the helicopter blades tossed them off course. Issa's magic and the carpet were no match for the devastating force churned from the machine.

"Let's get out of here!" Clip cried.

"I think Clip is right."

"For once," Aboo said to Issa.

Meanwhile, as the kids attempted to veer away from the oncoming helicopter and make their escape, the officers kept pace with them and gave chase. They were pursued aggressively, no matter how fast Issa pushed the flying carpet to travel, the chopper never fell back behind them.

"Identify yourselves or we'll shoot," a loud voice boomed from the aircraft.

"Oh no!" Issa cried to the other two genies. "What do we do?"

"Fly away," Aboo urged.

Wide-eyed, Issa turned away and banked hard to the left. The helicopter continued to give chase and then a bullet whizzed past her ear. They shot at them!

"Hold on tight!" she called to Clip and Aboo. As she pushed the flying carpet to its limits, it zoomed across the skies like a comet. The police officers working air patrol were left in their wake, completely dumbfounded. Their confused faces were the last thing she saw when she glanced over her shoulder until their ride carried them beyond reach of gunshot and into safety.

"Phew! That was a close one, Issa," Aboo said.

"You're telling me."

"At least we lost them," Clip said.

Issa glanced nervously over her shoulder again. Either the helicopter had no chance of catching up to them, or it had surrendered the chase altogether. She hoped it was the latter and that they didn't cross paths again. Her heart pounded in her chest and the adrenaline still flowed through her veins, making it hard to settle down and relax once imminent danger was over. "Something is telling me, this is not a friendly place," she commented.

"They didn't even offer us refreshments. Some hospitality," Clip muttered. His mind was on his snacks and food again as usual. The other two genies laughed and shook their heads as they gradually came down from their panic.

"Look down there!" Aboo pointed toward an area covered in twinkling lights full of amusement rides. Laughter from the crowds carried on the breeze and drew the genies toward the popular park.

"What is it?" Issa asked.

"I don't know, but that looks amazing!" Aboo cried out. "Let's go there and have fun."

"We can grab a bite to eat, too. I smell food."

"You always think of your stomach, Clip," Aboo laughed. "C'mon, Issa, please?

"Okay, but we must be careful," Issa cautioned.

The magic carpet descended and landed amidst a swarm of tourists gathered on Main Street. People in hats with mouse ears clapped upon their arrival, assuming they must have been part of the attractions. In their native clothes, the genies looked the part. People snapped photos of them, waved, and came up for autographs in their park themed signature books.

"Look, mommy! Look at the pretty birdie!" A young girl with a vanilla ice cream cone ventured close to the trio. Clip sidled down Issa's arm and made a snap at the frozen treat. The girl's mother caught her by the hand and tugged her out of reach.

"No stealing, Clip," Aboo chided in a quiet voice.

"I'm hungry."

"We'll get something later. Come on, let's go have some fun."

Issa grabbed Aboo's hand and pulled him through the festive crowd. They went from one ride to the next, screaming as they experienced their very first roller coaster ride. The haunted house made Aboo jump in fright, much to the delight of his companions, and the pirate themed attraction left them wanting to take a second ride.

"Look, a jungle cruise. I want to try this one next." Aboo said, leading the way.

The boat moved at a slow chug down the river through a swamp landscape that thickened into jungle. Animal roars and bird screeches blasted from concealed speakers and filled the air around them. Animatronic creatures peeked through the foliage as the drifted by.

"Oooh, fruit!" Clip hopped atop Aboo's head and snatched some berries from an overhanging branch. Hungry, he gobbled them up without a second glance, then promptly choked.

"Plastic!" he screeched in dismay as he spat the fake food out.

They followed their cruise with a ride on the famed monorail, passing through the various themed areas of the park. Aboo begged and pleaded until Issa agreed to ride another roller coaster with him. Space Mountain thrilled them. The genies followed the dark, galactic ride with snacks and then a visit to the large iconic castle in the park. Princesses in their colorful gowns waved from the balcony and blew kisses to the crowd.

"I want to go through the Haunted Mansion again before the park closes," Issa pleaded.

"I thought it scared you."

"No, it scared *you*," she told Aboo, tweaking his nose.

"Liar."

"Fine. Maybe it scared me a little. But it was fun."

They joined the non-existent queue and made their way inside, where they loaded up on one of the cars. The ride moved slowly, turning them left, right, forward, and back depending on what display deserved their focus. Ghostly apparitions danced in ballroom below and spooky groan filled the air.

A dark shape rose up amid the glowing gravestones. Artificial lightning flashed overhead, revealing Gengir Xul. Issa, Aboo, and Clip all cried out in fright.

"Let's get out of here!" Clip screeched.

Slipping out from behind the safety bar, the genies abandoned their car. Plastic grass crunched beneath their feet in their mad dash for escape. Animatronic skeletons cackled, strobing lights blinded them, and fog pumped out from hidden machines offered limited cover.

It wasn't enough.

"Gotcha!" Gengir Xul's clawed hand gripped Issa's shoulder from behind.

"Let me go," she shrieked. "Aboo, run!"

"Now you are mine."

"Not so soon, you creep!"

Fabric ripped as Issa struggled and freed herself from his grasp. She stumbled forward in time to see Aboo trip over a faux marble headstone. Rushing to the fallen genie, she grabbed him by the arm and pulled him up to his feet. Sizzling purple bolts flew over their heads. Aboo stumbled a second time, nearly pulling Issa down with him. Clip soared back to their pursuer and began pecking at Gengir Xul's head to buy his friends some time. The dark sorcerer tried to shoot him down with his magic bolts, but the parrot genie proved too agile.

A brilliant beam of energy shot past Clip and slammed into the wall. Everything began to shake and the ceiling above them buckled. Clip flew away with full haste, coughing and sputtering as the roof collapsed behind him.

"Hurry! Who knows how long that'll hold him!"

"Look, the exit!" Issa shouted. They ran for the door and burst outside into the cool night air.

"Get the carpet, get it now!" Clip cried. He settled on Issa's shoulder and shifted his weight from leg to leg in worry.

Aboo pulled the magical rug from his pocket and transformed it back to its normal size. He and Issa leapt on the moment it was rolled out and flew the carpet up into the sky. Only after the lights of the amusement park were behind them did they dare to relax.

"Are you all right, Aboo?" Issa checked her brother over.

"I'm fine, only a bruise or two. What of you? He grabbed you, Issa!"

"It's only a scratch," she reassured him. "What about you, Clip? You were amazing back there."

"Yes," Aboo agreed. "That was a great move, Clip. You saved our lives."

"Do I get a reward?"

Issa laughed. "When we get home, Clip."

"Which is where, exactly?"

"I..." Issa blinked.

Sharing the same thought, she and Aboo leaned forward and peered over the edge of the rug. In their hasty escape they had given no thought to which way they were going. Everywhere they looked the lights appeared the same.

"I'm not sure, Issa finished.

Clip huffed. "Oh great. We're lost."

"I'll get you home. Somehow..."

"That doesn't sound very reassuring."

"Give her a break, Clip. It's been a rough day for all of us."

"I was just wondering about my dinner, that's all."

Issa shot the parrot a dirty look but Aboo was the one who shook his head and snorted in disgust. "Always thinking about food."

"Sure. What else is there?"

Chapter 8

A large parlor had been transformed into the call center for Randy's brainchild. His 900 Genie phone line was raking in the cash. Honest and true digital currency he could be sure wouldn't disappear in a fit of genie pique or magical failure.

I'm absolutely brilliant, he congratulated himself, even while he seethed at the sight of three empty chairs. *Stupid kids, running off when there's work to be done.* The trio of genie youngsters would have to face some sort of disciplinary action for their behavior. In fact, Randy planned to punish all of them for shirking their duties. The kids should have known better, and the adults should have kept a closer eye on them.

Karim, Abdul, Salima, and Tamujin picked up the slack, but it still wasn't enough as far as Randy was concerned.

"I'm losing money right now." Scowling, Randy paced behind the four adult genies at their desks. He glanced down at his watch, huffed in irritation, then let loose a string of muttered profanities and complaints.

With Abo, Clip, and Issa gone the phones for the Master Junior and Master Pets went unanswered. Randy took it as a personal affront that the three had abandoned their posts.

"Are the four of us not enough?" Karim asked. "We can maintain the lines."

"Yeah, because you're doing such a bang up job at it," Randy snapped back. "Where are they? None of you are supposed to leave the house unless I will it."

"If they left, they're in great danger," Abdul replied.

Karim shook his head. He was either a good liar, or as clueless as the rest. "If Gengir Xul finds them, they're finished."

"We must search for them. There is no time to lose," Tamujin declared.

"Some genies you are. You can wish everything else into existence but you can't wish those three back here?"

"Our powers don't work that way," Abdul said.

Randy sneered at the small group of genies who remained. The obedient ones might have stayed in the house as ordered, but he didn't have any plans to lend them a helping hand. They could search for their misbehaving kin on their own without his help. "It looks like you have work to do," Randy said. He stormed out of the office.

***

"I have no idea which way to go." Issa fretted and peered over the carpet for the hundredth time.

"Great. We're lost. I knew it! Clip snapped his beak in agitation.

"Maybe we should get down and ask somebody," Aboo suggested.

"I guess..." Issa bit her lip, uncertain, but she guided the magic rug in for a landing. A street lamp flickered above them, revealing trash on the cracked road and graffiti on the walls. Two junked cars were parked up ahead.

"Excuse me, hello," Issa called out when she spotted a group gathered around one of the cars. Broken glass littered the road at their feet. "Hi, can you give us directions back to Beverly Hills?"

Five men spun away from the car and it became apparent they had been robbing the vehicle. One man held the torn out stereo in his hands and another stuffed a collection of loose change and dollar bills in his pockets. The other three aimed guns at the genies.

"Look what we have here, boys." Tattoos covered the arms of most of the men, but the one who stepped forward bore the heaviest ink. Flaming skulls and barbed wire decorated his biceps down to his wrists.

"Uh oh. This is bad." Clip tucked his wings close against his body and ruffled his feathers. The irritable grinding noise from his beak told them that Clip had reached the end of his rope. Too bad he wasn't able to do more than nip off a fingertip when motivated.

The gangsters moved forward and spread out until they circled the trio. Issa scooted closer to Aboo, grabbed his hand, and kept him close to her side.

"Look, we don't want trouble," she said. "Only directions."

The leader smirked. "The chick is mine, guys. Waste the kid. The bird, too. Maybe he'll make a good dinner."

"What? No!" Issa backed away and nearly stumbled over Aboo.

"The carpet! Get back on the carpet!" Clip screeched. "It's our only chance!"

"A dusty rug can't help you," one of the men laughed.

How wrong he was. Or would have been. The genies jumped on their magic carpet and urged it to lift off. The gang leader squashed the idea after a brief, startled glance, stamping his foot down on the rug with his heavy-booted foot.

"None of that now."

"Let me go!" Issa struggled in the leader's bruising grip.

Aboo rushed at the man with his fists up, bristling with fear and anger. "Leave her alone!"

The gang leader's fist connected with Aboo's jaw. The strike knocked the boy to the ground and sent bloodied spittle flying from his mouth.

"Aboo!" Issa screamed and tried to jerk away but the hand on her arm tightened.

"We're gonna have fun."

The leader pressed the muzzle of the handgun against Issa's cheek. While she wasn't familiar entirely with the modern world of mortals, she knew a weapon when she saw it and felt his sinister intent. A shudder went down her spine.

"Please don't," she pleaded.

With his other hand, he grabbed Issa's blouse and ripped it open, exposing her breasts to the cool night air. She screamed and raised both arms to shield her body from his view.

Another hoodlum kicked Aboo as he lie sprawled on the ground, curled in the fetal position. The toe of a sneaker struck him in the kidney and almost made the kid pee his pants. The pain was beyond anything he'd ever imagined in all of his life. Even as a genie, they'd been taken care of and spared the ills of the world. Their vessels provided their every need and protected them from danger.

If he could have granted his own wishes, he would have swept them all away from the armed men. Clip, appearing to have the same thought in mind, flew over the scene in circles. His frantic cries echoed down the alley.

"Help! Somebody help!" he called.

"Somebody waste that stupid bird," the leader ordered while wrenching Issa's arm away from her torso. He palmed her unprotected skin and stared down at her with a gloating expression. The hunger in his eyes terrified her more than Gengir Xul ever had.

"No! Don't hurt him! Please!" she pleaded as the thugs opened fire on Clip. A few bits of blue feather drifted through the air as he maneuvered in clever flight patterns. Clip's acrobatics saved him a .40 millimeter slug in the chest by mere inches.

Aboo fought weakly from the ground. Another thug, intrigued by the show between Issa and their leader, held him down by a foot to the neck while he watched. They waited their turn,

"Please, no, please."

"Shut up, whore." The cruel words preceded a slap that left Issa tasting blood in her mouth. Warm tears leaked from her eyes.

It was the worst experience of her entire life. Growing up she was used to men looking at her. They granted her compliments and offered her father treasures in exchange for her hand in marriage. They had begged for her, but they had never resorted to treatment like this.

With a hand twisted in her dark hair, the leader forced her to the ground. He dragged his rough hand up her thigh between her legs while she squirmed and cried. Issa had no idea where Clip was, or if he was even alive. She prayed he had gotten away. That he had gone for help.

"Hold her down for me, Crush. I want both my hands for this one."

The man he called Crush was a burly fellow with a shaved head and bulky muscles. The letters of his name were tattooed on his knuckles, a detail Issa noticed when he pinned her arms against the dirty asphalt.

"Don't be greedy boss, save some for us," one of the men called out. The stout young man with the sagging pants leered at Issa. He held a half empty beer bottle in one hand, which he raised to his lips and swigged from before spitting a mouthful on her.

"This one's lively, there's plenty to go around. Isn't there, pretty?"

A tall, dark figure stepped from the shadows. Aboo's terrified gasp broke through Issa's own sobbing cries. She turned her head and spotted Gengir Xul through her tears. Somehow, even he seemed the lesser of two evils in this moment. At least he would make the end for her quick. Maybe even painless.

"Hey man, who the hell do you think you are? Get out of here," saggy pants yelled.

Gengir Xul didn't even look at the gang member. The dark sorcerer extended his hand and threw the man across the road on a blast of purple light.

"The genies are mine." His voice, while low, boomed down the empty street like the rumbling bass of thunder.

"Shit!"

The gangsters opened fire on Gengir Xul, gunshots filling the night. Their bullets proved useless and bounced off the sorcerer. The smell of urine became overwhelming as one man pissed himself when their clips emptied and their victim remained standing. Unharmed.

"Man, we gotta get out of here. C'mon, dawg, we can't be stayin' up in this place. This dude bulletproof like Superman!"

"No." After the gang leader reloaded his handgun, he aimed the glock at the sorcerer again. "This is my hood. And I'm not leaving it for some trick in fancy clothes. He better get to steppin' if he thinks I'm leavin' my shit to him."

The pensive faces of his fellow gangbangers all looked around the dark alley. Their guns weren't enough to take out a man who was impervious to bullets. The kids weren't worth it. No amount of money in all of the world could make them worth the danger that Gengir Xul exuded.

Sirens screamed from around the corner and then flashing lights appeared at the end of the street. Nervous, the gangbangers all exchanged looks with one another but their leader, resolute in his decision, stood firm and refused to budge.

"Let's show the cops why they don't come around here anymore."

***

Detective Rick Connor nudged the turn signal and turned onto the next street. With home a few blocks away and just around the corner, he was eager to hit the shower and crawl into bed. Considering the vast amount of strange activities occurring in the city, he had deserved the chance to rest. Tomorrow would mark a new day, and a new chance to get to the bottom of the investigation troubling the LAPD.

Only days ago, a mad man had blown up one of their detention centers, injuring and killing several of his fellow officers of the law. The unforgivable crime meant that someone had to pay, and he couldn't let his guard down until someone was brought to justice.

"578 to Central. We are on Lexington and Ward. Need reinforcements."

Rick glanced at the street sign on the corner. With the location barely a few miles out of his way, he had all of the time he needed to arrive on the scene.

"I'll be right there," he said into the radio.

Rick tapped a button on the dash and activated his lights. They whirled and turned rapidly, emitting the telltale red, white, and blue associated with the police. He grinned as the alarm whooped and the traffic parted to allow him through. He blazed through a series of intersections and red lights until he reached his destination minutes later.

A half dozen of LA's finest parked adjacent to the scene and left their vehicles. By the time Rick left the car, a cop had the megaphone ready for him. The cops took their stances with their weapons, poised and ready to shoot.

"Drop your guns," Rick ordered, using his most authoritative tone. "You are surrounded."

Chapter 9

The gang leader kept a tight grip on Issa's hair. She winced as he used it as a tether to pull her to her feet. She held the tattered remnants of her blouse together, mournfully sniffling. Tears left a glistening trail upon her swollen cheek, and the stinking smell of cheap beer left its odor on her black hair.

Gengir Xul appeared at his side, wearing a victorious expression on his features. Overjoyed, he glanced from the subjugated boy genie to the injured bird. The girl had grown and filled out since he last saw her, more beautiful than he'd ever dreamed.

"We are on the same side," he spoke to the gang leader.

"In this hood, I call the shots. Who do you think you are? Ali Baba?"

"Let me handle this," Gengir Xul said.

The meddling bird swooped toward the police force. One of the officers jerked back, a startled expression on his face.

"Help! Help!" Clip cried.

With the ease of swatting a fly, Gengir raised his hand and aimed his palm at Clip. A purple beam imbued with mystical force struck the bird and knocked him to the ground at the leading cop's feet. The parrot skidded against the unforgiving asphalt, scraping blue feathers from his wings.

"Shit! Take cover!" one of the gang members cried. Without a choice but to seek refuge behind dumpsters and out of the way, they bore witness to a magical assault. Gengir's roar shook the very asphalt beneath them. They staggered as they ran for cover and searched for places to hide despite their leader's orders to stand against the police.

Lightening flashed in the dark, and each branching bolt of electricity sizzled into the police cars before them. The chaotic scene only worsened as a police car exploded and its officers scattered.

"We need reinforcements! Choppers, medical aid, everything!" Rick screamed into his radio. The detective raced for the entrance to the run down building and kicked in the door. Years of practice on the SWAT team had given him an excellent advantage over accessing almost any domicile.

"What's happening?" asked a concerned resident. A woman in hair curlers and a robe peeked out of her door.

"Gang shoot out, ma'am. Close your doors and lock them!" Rick called to her.

Her prompt response was to slam the door. The deadbolt clicked into place as he sped up the stairs. Other residents of the apartment opened their doors and peered out, worried faces gazing back at him through the dimly lit halls of the poorly structure slum building.

"Close your doors! Gang shootout in progress!" he shouted to them.

By the time he reached the top of the stairs and burst out onto the roof access, reports spilled in through his radio that more officers were down. He moved to the ledge and aimed his gun at the gang leader. Paco Valdez had been in and out of the LA detention center for years, and as much as Rick wanted to send him away again for good, he didn't have any choice about taking him in alive. The gangbanger had a hostage.

Rick took the shot. Down below, Paco jerked and released his victim. As he stumbled back, the girl scrambled away to safety. Rick aimed his gun at Gengir Xul and squeezed the trigger to no avail. The bullet popped off the sorcerer's temple like a penny tossed at a steel wall.

Gengir Xul retaliated with a streak of lightning. Raw power flew from his fingertips and struck Rick along with the building in a storm of electricity. The building trembled and shook as Rick fell through the collapsing roof. The rest of the building began to crumble.

Chapter 10

So now what am I supposed to do with these kids? Rick wondered. He sat on the edge of his desk, facing the two youngsters from the violent attack in the 'hood. The forced smile on his face pressed his willpower to the limit, but he didn't want to appear to be an intimidating force after the kids suffered their own terrifying ordeal. They were all fortunate to be alive.

The young woman, survivor of a near sexual assault attempt, wore a spare blouse from a female officer's locker. It hung off of her slight frame. The younger child beside her sported his own number of scrapes and bruises.

Like the kids, Rick was fortunate to escape the incident with his life. Their bird occupied his lap, looking rough around the edges and missing a few feathers.

Sergeant Ramirez appeared at the door and leaned into the office. "We lost them, sir."

"Search the entire area. I want twenty-four hour surveillance on everything there. It looks like the same guy that blasted his way out of the detention center last week. It was like something out of a superhero flick, only we all faced the villain."

"Yes, sir."

After Ramirez left, Rick turned to face Issa. Watching her, he realized she wasn't as youthful as he initially thought.

"You were lucky," he said to her.

"I know. Thank you. You risked your life for us." Her eyes, bright as earth-toned jewels, shimmered when their eye contact held. Rick couldn't recall the last time he saw a woman so beautiful despite the scratches and nicks on her cheeks.

"It's my job," Rick said.

The little boy glanced between them. His mischievous smile distracted Rick from admiring Issa's fair looks.

"Huh?" the bird squawked. "Haven't we seen that look before?"

Rick glanced down at the parrot in his lap. He stared in amazement while the creature ruffled his dirty feathers. The animal may have needed a bath, but his complete sentence wasn't the first time Rick witnessed such a display of intelligence from him.

"You wouldn't by any chance have a little something to eat?" asked Clip.

"Uh. Yeah, sure." He'd marvel over the bird's uncanny intellect later. For now, he set Clip aside on the desk and maneuvered behind it to open a drawer. He fetched out a package of crackers, the graham kind always dispensed in hospitals, and ripped open the plastic. Clip fell on the pair of sweet honey wheat wafers like a hawk.

"So..." Rick glanced back at Issa and Aboo. "You were reported missing last night. Your family is on their way."

Ramirez arrived again. "The party's arrived, sir."

Randy filled the doorway next once Ramirez stepped aside. His older brother, ever the waste of space criminal, glowered into the office at the two kids.

"You!?" Rick demanded. He leapt to his feet. Heat pounded in his head as the beginning of a migraine lurked just behind his eyeballs. Whenever he had to deal with Randy for long, they always returned.

"He is not our family!" Issa cried.

"Hello, little brother," Randy said. "I'm a respectable businessman now."

"Respectable? You? I highly doubt that." Instinct made him reach behind behind his back for his handcuffs. He paused and dropped both arms down to his sides.

"That's right. You can't arrest me. I didn't break the law."

Rick scoffed and glanced at the Issa and Aboo. He had to wonder what a nice young woman and sweet kid like him were doing with his lowlife older brother Randy. "Not yet, but it won't be too long."

"Just watch me."

"Believe me, I will. It's my job to keep pricks like you in line. You'll never amount to anything. You're always going to be a waste on the system, Randy. And when you mess up again, I'll be there to see it happen."

Aboo and Issa left their seats. The latter gathered Clip into her arms and they filed out of the office door to join Randy. She flashed a smile over one shoulder at Rick and disappeared into the hallway.

***

"I am so glad you are all safe." Karim released his hold on Issa then pulled Aboo into his embrace. Salima took Issa by the hand and stroked her other palm over the girl's battered cheek.

"We were so worried about you," Salima told them.

"Yeah, well, if you'd listened to the rules none of this would have happened." Randy tossed his coat aside on the back of the couch, not seeming to care when it fell to the floor. "In the future, under no circumstances, are you to ever leave this house without my express permission."

Issa stepped forward, pulling free of Salima's comforting arms. "You do not own us," she hissed. "We are not your slaves."

"Actually, yes I do and yes, you are."

"He is right about leaving the house," Karim interjected, stepping between Issa and Randy. He settled his hands on the genie's quaking shoulders and gave them a gentle squeeze. "Issa, it is dangerous out there, as you have learned. Next time you might not be so lucky. Do you all understand?"

Issa, Aboo, and Clip all hung their heads.

"We only went sightseeing," Aboo mumbled.

"This is not the old times, my children, and you are not Sinbad." Salima's kind smile took any sting out of her words.

"Don't do it again." Randy glared at them all before he turned around and strode from the room.

"I like it here better anyway." Clip flew from Aboo's shoulder over to the side table where date filled platters filled his attention. "At least there's plenty of food."

***

The expansive warehouse held a gritty atmosphere, the stale smell of chemicals thick in the air and oil stains on the floor. They ran their drug operation and sometimes their prostitution jobs out of the warehouses many rooms, and with the LAPD in such a disarray, they had no doubt that they'd be able to continue with their new leader at the helm.

Gengir Xul examined his new headquarters with an air of authority. Gangbangers led him around the many rooms and explained their practices.

"We run all our business from here," Crush said.

"It needs some remodeling," Gengir Xul muttered. He stroked his chin, wearing a thoughtful expression. His eyes narrowed then swept to the side to fixate on the other thug. "It needs something special."

"Just tell us what to do, Boss," Martinez said.

"I want my genies first, and then maybe I'll just take over your world."

The gang members looked at each other. Slowly, they began to grin.

"Awesome. Tell us what to do to make it happen, man." Crush and Martinez touched fists and eagerly waited for instructions.

MARIA COWEN

Chapter 11

Bacon sizzled on the stove and waffled popped up from a nearby toaster. Kimberly moved around her modest kitchen, trying her best not to trip over the dogs or her son.

"Where did that other dog come from again?" she asked, irritated by the non-stop activity. "You know you're not supposed to let in strays, kiddo."

"Floppy called the wish line for pets, mom, like I told you." Luke wore his Orange Power Ninja suit and flipped across the room, kicking off the wall and touching the ceiling in his acrobatic display.

"This place is too small for two dogs."

"But look, they're so happy together," Luke gushed.

Kim huffed out a frustrated breath, closed her eyes, and pinched the bridge of her nose. *Breathe, Kimmy, just breathe. Five... Four... Three... Two... One...* Her headache ebbed but didn't dissipate entirely.

"I know they do, hon," she began, trying to keep calm. Behind her, the bacon began to smoke. "But soon we'll have a house full of puppies and then what'll we do?"

Floppy and his unnamed companion dashed through the kitchen in another round of chase. This time their playful antics brought them in too close to Kimberly's legs and she nearly tripped over them on her way to rescue the bacon.

"Ugh! I've *had* it with these two!"

"Please, Mom!"

Kimberly ignored her son and reached for the phone after she turned off the stove. She had been too late for the bacon. All that remained were charred strips. She punched the number in for 900 Genie and drummed her perfectly manicured nails against the counter.

"All our genies are assisting other callers, but if you remain on the line the first available--"

Kimberly slammed the receiver down on the automated voice. "I don't have time for this right now. On top of that, I have to go over to that house again."

"The big fancy one?" Luke latched on to the change in topic, eager to shift focus away from the dogs.

"Yeah, that one up in Beverly Hills." Kimberly tipped the burnt bacon into the trash.

"Can I come with you? It sounds cool and I promise to be good."

She smeared butter over the cooled waffles then passed one over to Luke while she munched on the other. *Should I bring him? It's not exactly professional but it would give me an excuse to go in and get out quickly. That guy gives me the creeps. All of them do.* "Fine, but you'll stay in the car, understood?"

"Thanks, Mom. Ninja Power!"

Sighing, she shook her head. It was going to be a long day ahead of her, no matter how she cut it.

"Get the dogs put away in the garage with fresh water while I get cleaned up, then we'll go."

"Sure thing, mom. I'll take care of them."

Her son hopped up without hesitation and chased after the dogs. Kim couldn't help but smile at his hasty assistance. *I guess we'll have to name the other one. But later, not right now.* She hurried off to straighten up her mussed hair and reapply her lipstick. Once everything was ready, she locked up the apartment and ushered her son to the car.

Why do I feel like I'm going to some sort of horror attraction? It's only a house. An expensive, gorgeous, richly decorated house... But still. Just a house.

Thirty minutes later they pulled up the long driveway of the mansion and parked the car. Kim put the vehicle in park but left the keys in the ignition on the off-chance she had to make a mad getaway. After the last visit, she didn't plan to leave anything up to chance and didn't trust the creepster homeowner not to leer at her again.

"Luke, I'm going in. You stay in your seat with your game and don't touch anything, okay? I'll be right back. Just stay here in the car. Honk if you have to."

"Okay, Mom." Luke smiled from the back seat.

Kim shut the door behind her, though she briefly contemplated leaving it open too and decided that was overkill. She dashed up the steps down the immaculate path winding between the halves of the immaculate front lawn and rang the bell.

The door creaked open to reveal a ghoulish face staring down at her. Lips curled into a perpetual snarl pulled back from fanged teeth, lending a feral appearance to the tall man before her. Kimberly shrank back and gasped, and in doing so, nearly toppled off the stoop. The man, tall and powerful as he was built, with broad shoulders and a strong, athletic build, reached out to steady her.

"No need to worry," the tall man said. "Please come in."

"Oh, yes. Thank you." *Chin up, Kimmy. You're a professional.* So why did she feel like turning and running for her car like a scared teen at their first haunted house?

Her mental pep-talk helped. She took one step after the other, her three-inch heels clicking on the marble floor as she followed the intimidating man through the entry hall. He led her into the same living room as before, as fancy and colorful as she remembered from her first visit.

"By the way, you look stunning today."

"I... oh, um, thank you." The compliment, so genuine in its offering, eased some of her discomfort. "It's because of that 900 Genie line."

"Yes, I know." A small smile tugged up the corners of his mouth.

Kimberly blinked. "You do? But how?"

"I am the one who granted you your wish."

She froze before she had a chance to sit on the plush couch, then turned and stared at him. "*You're* the genie?"

"Yes. My name is Tamujin."

What a strange name, she thought. "So... can you grant any wish?"

"Almost. There are certain limitations, even for us. I could not, for example, kill anyone for you, or make someone love you."

"Oh, see." More relaxed, she took a seat on the sofa

and even dared to accept one of the honeyed pastries Tamujin offered her from a silver tray. "What if, say, I wanted to meet the man of my life?"

"Perhaps you already have," Tamujin replied with another of his small smiles.

"What do you mean by that? I'm fairly certain I'd know, wouldn't I?"

"Well... The first time I saw you, Miss Kimberly, you reminded me so much of--"

"You?" Kim interrupted, stunned. "Oh no, you can't be serious." *Look at him. He has fangs for god sake, and he looks sort of like a bear with that fur growing around his ears down to his chin.*

Tamujin bowed his head. "My... condition is temporary. I did not always look as you see me now."

A sense of unease crept over Kimberly's body. She cleared her throat and said nothing about what he said, instead turning to her briefcase. She unsnapped the top with trembling fingers and pulled out the paperwork.

"Mr. Connor missed a signature spot here on page five. We can't proceed with the deed transfer without it."

"He is not in right now, but I will ensure he signs it the moment he steps inside."

"Perfect. I'll swing back by this afternoon then so we can finish this all up." *God, I don't want to come back out here again.*

"I will walk you out."

This time as they walked down the hall, Kimberly caught the sound of many ringing phones. Catching her interest, Tamujin gestured her to silence and opened a side door. Inside the room Kimberly noted several desks, each with their own phone. Five people manned the lines and each wore a matching expression of boredom.

"Is that where the calls come in for 900 Genie?" Kim asked after Tamujin closed the door back up.

"Yes. All calls come in there. Four of us for the main line, two for the juniors, and one for the pets."

"Seriously? Pets can't call on the phone." Yet she had a female collie in her house at that very moment who proved otherwise.

Tamujin only smiled in his way and led her to the door, where he opened it for her like a true gentleman. Kimberly almost returned the smile, until she spotted a scene that made her heart stop.

Her car was empty.

"Oh my god, Luke!"

Kimberly rushed outside and nearly tripped over her heels in her haste. Panic swept over her while a thousand possibilities ran through her mind.

"Oh man, this is great! Look at me, Mom!"

Her son's voice drew her frantic gaze upward and she nearly fainted on the spot. Luke was flying on a carpet, like someone out of a fairy tale.

"Luke, you get down here right now!"

"He is quite safe, I promise." A new voice made Kim spin around. There, leaning against the trunk of the car, was a boy who looked to be near Luke's age. His arms were crossed over his chest and a bright smile lit up his entire face as he watched her son soaring overhead. "He is a natural."

The carpet zipped through the air, doing loops and

fast-paced dives. Kimberly gasped, heart pounding, and instinctively grabbed for Tamujin's hand. *Please, oh God, I can't lose Luke. I just can't.* The mere thought was torturous.

"He will be fine," Tamujin reassured her in a soft voice. He squeezed her hand and smoothed his thumb over her knuckles. "They are only having fun Miss Kimberly."

No, no it is not all right. He'll get hurt. "Get down right this instant!" she shrieked.

"Man, you ruin everything," Luke called down. He guided the magic carpet down into a sharp, fast descent that had Kim's breath catching in her chest and her heart skipping a beat.

"See?" Tamujin told her. "No harm done."

"We need to go. I... we can't stay."

"I will be waiting for you." A wet spot remained after Tamujin kissed her knuckles. His grotesque teeth didn't allow him to shut his mouth, which gave Tamujin the appearance of a Japanese angry demon mask. Kimberly shuddered and tugged her hand away and spun on her heels. She snagged Luke away from the younger genie to push him into the car. She didn't even wait for him to buckle his seatbelt before she peeled out of the drive.

Chapter 12

"Mooooom, I was having fun," Luke protested from the back seat. He whined and he cried like a spoiled brat in the rear of the seat, while all Kimberly wanted to do was to wash her hands of that weird man's spit. She'd never considered herself to be a snob before, but deep down, she knew no amount of kind words and manners could let her ignore that face.

Maybe it was a face only a mother could love, but as a mother, Kimberly had to disagree. She shuddered again behind the wheel and hit the turn signal.

"We're going to make a stop at the grocery store to pick up some eggs," she said.

"Awwww. Do I have to go in?"

"Yes."

"But I don't want to get out the car and it's not hot outside."

In a matter of seconds, Kimberly could imagine exiting the supermarket to find a gaggle of good samaritans standing outside of her car. She pictured the shards of glass from her window on the floor and some officer taking off his handcuffs to take her to jail.

"Nuh un, buddy. You're coming in with me. What if some bad grown-up tries to take you away?"

Luke made a few exaggerated kung-fu sound effects and karate chopped the air. "Nobody can kidnap me now, Mom! I'm a power ninja."

"Good point."

She parked the vehicle and turned in her seat to stare at her son. "Look, just like at the mansion, you stay put and don't touch anything. I'm going to crack the windows and lock the doors, then I'll be back in five minutes. Ten tops."

"Ninja's honor, I'll be good."

Kimberly bypassed the carts in favor of a handbasket. The tactic kept her from wandering and overbuying. A quick in and out was what she wanted.

"I called a second time. Dad's been sober ever since."

Two nearby stock girls chatted together while they loaded canned soup onto a shelf. Neither one paid Kimberly any mind as they shared gossip.

"Yeah? I called too and look, I have my hair back. It's better than ever before."

"I still can't believe that stylist mangled it so badly. It looks amazing, Tisha."

"Totally. That 900 Genie is amazing."

Kimberly grabbed some tomato soup and hurried out of the aisle. She didn't want to even think of the hotline, but there was no escaping it. Voices drifted up the breakfast aisle, this time from two middle aged women Kim recognized from Luke's school.

"I swear, Janet, Harvey and I didn't do it for months. After I called that line he became an absolute stallion and he can't get enough of me. Why, just yesterday we made love in his truck like a pair of teen agers right before my shift at work."

Ew. Not what I wanted to know about the lunch lady, Kimberly thought. She skipped grabbing cereal, fetched the eggs she came in for, and then headed for check out. Even the cashier gushed about the genies, ringing up Kim's few items while carrying on about her new pay raise thanks to her call.

Kim couldn't get outside fast enough, and she almost left her eggs behind in her haste. Crossing the lot to her car, a sudden sense of wrong engulfed her, and it took only a quick glance to tell her the problem.

Luke was gone.

***

Luke watched his mom head into the store and wished she had left her keys so he could at least play the radio. Bored, he stared out the window.

"Man, this sucks, the boy mumbled. "I should have gone inside. Maybe she'd get me a candy bar."

"Hey, sweetie."

Luke jumped at the sound of his mother's voice and twisted to look at the door opposite his. His mom stood on the other side of the door with a smile and a wave.

"Geez, Mom, you scared me. I didn't even see you come out."

"Come with me."

He didn't have to be asked twice. Whooping in excitement, Luke unbuckled and opened his door. His mom rounded the car, took him hand in a firm hold, and started tugging for him to follow. In fact, her grip on his hand hurt a little.

"Mom, the store's back that way."

"This way." Her grip tightened.

"Mom, what's wrong? You're scaring me." Luke tried to tug his hand free. Ahead, a motley assortment lurked around an old van with rust spots on the side. One man was playing with a knife and another had a gun tucked into his belt.

In an instant, it was no longer his mother dragging him toward the gangsters. Her pretty features melted away, replaced with dark hair and red eyes. The hand around his arm elongated into sharp claws.

"Take him," Gengir Xul ordered.

"No!" Luke yelled. Dozens of hands reached for him, prompting the boy to raise his arms in order to protect his face. Bright orange filled his vision -- his Power Ninja suit.

I can do this. I'm strong. I'm a superhero.

Bolstered by the reminder of his powers, Luke leaped into the air. He ripped from their grips, somersaulted over their heads, and kicked two gang members before he touched back down to the ground. It was a performance worthy of a black belt martial artist.

Luke spun on his heel and kicked straight out, slamming his foot into the knife wielder's jaw, then he flipped away out of reach. Laughter bubbled up inside as he played a game of duck and dodge with his attempted kidnappers. They were too slow.

"Shit, man, this crazy kid hits hard." Crush rubbed his aching jaw.

"Imbeciles." Gengir Xul stepped forward. ""I shall take care of this."

"You better man," Crush said. "I hope we didn't call you boss for nothing. This is loco."

That guy's the boss. The villain. I can get him. "Ninja Power!" Luke sprinted forward and leapt into the air. The time to attack was now. He had to get away and get back to him mom. More than anything, he had to protect her.

Gengir Xul lifted his hands, palms out and claw-tipped fingers bent inwards. Luke thought he looked exactly like the bad guy from his favorite science fiction movie when he was about to shoot lightning from his hands.

No electrical arcs came, but something did happen.

He fell.

Mid-flip Luke's orange ninja suit vanished and with it, his powers. Instead of landing on his feet ready to kick ass and take names, the boy belly-flopped onto the men he was trying to leap over.

"Wow, how'd you do that boss?" Crush asked.

"I did not." Gengir Xul's brows furrowed and his eyes narrowed in thought. "Restrain the boy. We have what we came for."

"No, you can't do this to me! Mom! *Mom!*" Luke screamed. He struggled and kicked but he was only a weak kid without his powers. They used rough rope to bind his wrists and ankles, and someone stuffed a rag in his mouth to muffle his cries.

The last thing he remembered was being tossed into the van head first, then the world went dark.

Chapter 13

Angry phone calls poured in over 900 Genie' phone lines. Abdul, Karim, Salima, Issa, and Clip struggled to keep up with the calls and reassure their clients. Not that they were going to see a single penny of the money that Randy had acquired since they came into his service. He was nothing better than a slave driver who overworked them at all hours of the day. They were no better off free from their vessels.

"...and suddenly it all went 'poof!' Just disappeared into thin air. I want my money back!" one customer demanded, shrieking into the phone.

"You cheated me. I want my money back right now," another client told them. The endless calls were all some variance of the same chief complaint.

"...I had everything I wanted, and now it's all gone. What kind of business are you running out there?!"

"I've never been so happy before. Now she won't even look at me."

"I've been so proud of myself. Now it's the size of my pinky finger again."

"I'm three hundred pounds once more. None of my new dresses fit."

"He doesn't love me anymore, now that he sees I'm eighty years old. I'm going to die of a broken heart."

"...It's a rip-off! Fraud! I'll call the authorities. We want a refund."

"...my open mind doesn't do me any good now."

"...my hair is all gone! I thought it was going to last."

"What's going on?" Randy stepped inside rubbing his hands together. "Hot damn, we're getting another spike. I'll be set for the rest of my life."

Karim shook his head. "Quite the opposite. We have had thousands of complaints. People are asking for refunds and will want their money back."

"Come again?" Randy's grin flipped into a scowl.

"The wishes don't hold," Salima explained. Our magic fades after a certain time."

"Now my clients just bark and howl and screech at me," Clip lamented.

"But why?" Issa asked. "Why isn't it working anymore?"

"I don't know. You tell me. It's *your* job. Randy crossed his arms over his chest and tapped his foot against the floor. "Well? I'm waiting. I'm not going to lose my business and all of my new riches because all of you don't want to do your jobs correctly."

"Maybe because it is second hand magic," Karim suggested.

Randy whipped his head toward the genie. "What do you mean?"

"You are our master. We can fulfill your wishes only." Abdul bowed his head.

"But you're wishing that we grant wishes to others," Issa pointed out, catching on. "So that makes those wishes second hand."

"Whatever it is, it's good for us," Randy decided. A sinister grin spread over his face. Greed took its hold and lit his blue eyes up with happiness.

"Good? How?" Salima asked.

Randy chuckled. Their confusion didn't faze him. "Repeat business. They'll have to come back for more, every time it fades. It's hard to let go of a good thing, once you taste it. It'll be like crack. Nobody will be able to call for just one hit. We'll make even more money now that we know how much they're willing to pay for this service."

"Oh no!" Clip cried.

Their master remained either oblivious to their fears, or too ignorant to grasp the danger of his new edict. "I'll keep you very busy, my friends." Randy smirked.

Tears welled in Salima's eyes. "Why are you doing this to us?"

Karim leapt to his feet. His family would never have suffered so greatly at Randy's hands if he didn't drag them into his dilemma. If he'd known Randy only intended to use them as free slave labor, he would have allowed them to remain in their vessels and merely smuggled them back to the mansion. "You don't need money. We can give you more than you can ever spend."

"That's not good enough," Randy said. "I want vengeance. I want to see my brother suffer. Grant me my wish, or you'll slave in 900 mines forever."

"This is blackmail!" Issa shoved away from her desk.

"Call it what you want, sweetheart. I don't care."

"Master, we cannot do as you ask." Salima moved closer to Issa and wrapped an arm around the furious girl.

"As we have told you, we can't intentionally harm anyone. We certainly can't kill." Karim struggled to maintain his calm. If he lost control then his family would have no one to be strong for them.

"Why not, huh? You're genies. You have the power to make anything happen. Who cares if you squash one pathetic looser?"

"No," Abdul said, plain and simple.

Salima picked up where her companion left off. "What you are asking involves evil. Remember our code of ethics?"

"To hell with ethics!" Randy roared He picked up a chair and threw it across the room into the buffet table. Dates, pastries, and single serving meat pies went flying everywhere across the room, an explosion of edible goodies to be cleaned by his genie wait staff.

"Master..." Karim stepped forward while the rest of his family flinched back from Randy's rage. "We cannot delve into the dark side. It simply cannot be done."

"Fine. Issa and Karim, handle the complaints. No refunds. The rest of you, get back to work!"

Randy stormed out of the office and slammed the door behind him.

"I want to go back to my jar," Clip said in a quiet, despairing voice.

No one could blame him.

***

Rick's expression became the very model of sympathy for the young woman in the chair. As she finished off the last

Kleenex in the box on his desk, he fetched a replacement from a drawer and leaned forward to offer it to her. She took it, a grateful and forced half-smile on her face.

"Thank you." Amidst her sniffles, she'd tried to tell him what happened. It was a regrettable situation that could happen to almost any parent. Or rather, only to foolish parents who left their young children alone in a parked vehicle. Rick tried not to judge, and thankfully years on the force gave him the experience to school his expressions and put out neutral conversation. Professionalism was key. Chastising her wouldn't bring the boy back, and she certainly had learned her lesson not to do it again.

"Do you know the whereabouts of the child's father?"

"He works overseas... Kuwait."

Damn. It wasn't the kid's father who took him then. Had to be someone else. Maybe someone she knows, Rick thought. He made a few notes on a separate pad then returned to filling out the disappearance report. "That puts him out of the picture. Is there anyone else in Luke's life right now who may have an interest in taking him?"

"No..." Kimberly pursed her lips, remained silent a moment, then shook her head again in confirmation. "No, there's nobody."

"All right. The report is filled out. We'll make sure that an Amber Alert goes out."

"Can I do anything to help?"

"Just go home and remain calm. We'll call you as soon as we have news."

***

How can I just go home when my baby is missing? I can't sit and do nothing. I have to look for him I... I have to find him somehow. Kimberly's dry eyes stung and fresh tears welled to the surface.

Mr. Connor's mansion rose up before her, but she honestly didn't recall meaning to drive there. Her car rolled to a stop and she set the parking brake, fingers tight on the wheel and her emotions a mess.

They're genies. If anyone can help me find my Luke it's them. Right?

Mind made up she left the car before second thoughts deterred her. One deep breath and then she pressed her trembling finger against the doorbell button. Once. Twice. She rang it a third time and held the button down.

The door swung open on its own, reminding Kimberly of spooky events from a recent horror movie. Under ordinary circumstances, she would have balked and fled back to her car. Not today. She stepped inside and made her way down the only hallway she was familiar with until she reached the living room.

Two men sat on a low couch playing cards. Tamujin was the only one whose name she knew, but the other rang a bell in her memory. He had been there the first day when she came with all the paperwork for the house. Unfinished take-out pizza on the coffee table looked out of place in the exotic room.

"Miss Kimberly."

Tamujin leapt to his feet and, without a thought, Kim rushed for him. She fell into his arms and wept.

"He's gone! My son is gone and I don't know where he is."

"What?"

"Luke," she sobbed. "I ran into the store and when I came out he was gone. I was only inside for a few minutes, I swear."

Tamujin guided her over toward the couch and nudged her to take a seat. "Perhaps Karim and I can help you find him."

"Oh could you? Really?" Kim swiped at her cheeks and looked between both men. "I'm so scared and the police said they'd look but... But what if he's been kidnapped? What if he's hurt somewhere after doing all those flips?"

"Do you have a picture of your son?" Karim asked. His kind eyes reassured her.

Kimberly dug through her purse and pulled out her wallet. Her fingers shook as she unsnapped the buckle on the purple pleather billfold. The clear plastic sleeves were all filled with photographs from over the years. Her little boy, from birth to now, she had a picture from each year of his life.

"Here," she whispered as she passed over the most recent photo. Luke's school picture had him in front of a green background that clashed with his favorite orange shirt.

"Thank you." Karim accepted the photo and set it in his lap before he conjured up a small silver framed mirror. Kim watched, both awed and fearful.

Magic. I still can't believe it.

Yet she knew it was real. Magic and a genie's wish had given her, albeit briefly, a figure that stopped traffic. All that was gone now but she didn't care. Only Luke mattered.

Karim muttered word in a foreign language and waved his hand over the mirror. The reflective surface began to glow and a mist swirled over the top. Tamujin's hand on her back moved in soothing strokes which slowed her racing heart.

"Look, it's working," Tamujin whispered.

Kimberly leaned forward and looked into the picture playing out in the mirror.

Chapter 14

The sorcerer and his flunkies had bundled Luke up like a sausage with more ropes than Houdini could untie. He sat on the filthy floor, leaning against the wall with dried tears leaving clean streaks on his dirt-smudged face.

Gengir Xul paced up and down the floor while debating his next plan of action. Everything was falling into place. Given a little more time, he'd have the genies back in his possession. And then the world would be his. He chuckled quietly, too pleased with his ideas to pay any mind to Crush following on his heels.

"What do you want to do with the little brat? We don't have a babysitter," Crush said.

Gengir Xul growled and stopped. The abrupt halt led to his underling bumping into him. "Watch your step, you moron!"

Crush fell back a few steps as the sorcerer's pacing resumed. It took ten seconds before their accident was repeated. This time Gengir Xul zapped Crush with an arc of purple energy. A few of the others laughed at their gang leader's sharp yelp and dazed expression as he stumbled back. Luke trembled and tried his best to curl into a ball.

"Sorry, boss," Crush wheezed.

"Imbecile," Gengir Xul muttered with a sneer. He

resumed his pacing unhindered, a thousand thoughts and possibilities running through his head. He needed the genies and, despite his disgust for their inferior lives, he needed the humans with their guns and modern day know-how. But how to get what he wanted?

His eyes cut toward the snot-faced whelp and a slow smile curved his thin, bloodless lips. "I have a plan."

***

Kimberly sobbed into a handkerchief. "My boy. They have my baby boy."

"It couldn't be worse," Karim mused, rubbing his chin.

Tamujin shook his head and fixed Karim with a stern glance. "The boy could be dead. Things could be worse."

Another shuddering sob wracked Kimberly's shoulders, prompting Tamujin to put his arm around her.

"You are right. Please forgive my pessimistic outlook, Kimberly," Karim said in apology.

"We'll help you," Tamujin assured her. Concern lined his heavy brow.

"You will? Do you promise?" Kim sat up and grabbed Tamujin's shoulders. Her fingers curled into his shirt. "Luke is everything I've got. I'm not even pretty anymore."

The large genie stroked Kim's blonde hair back from her face. "Oh, yes, you are. Actually, I like you better this way. You're more natural." She'd looked like a Barbie doll before, all plastic and makeup without any substance. In her natural state, Kimberly wasn't hard on the eyes. Her features, while striking and lovely, couldn't be described as gorgeous, but she certainly caught Tamujin's eye.

The door swung open with enough force that it smacked against the wall, leaving a dent in the painted plaster where the doorknob struck. The noise startled both genies and the woman in their company, all three leaping to their feet. Randy strutted into the room flanked by two women on each side of his body, a cocky grin on his face. His companions were all stunning in appearance, dressed for a night on the town in skin-tight dresses that left nothing to the imagination.

"Champagne!" Randy called out. "I wish for lots of champagne, this fancy French shit that no one can afford, and... are you girls hungry?" Giggles and nods were his reply. The redhead hanging on his left arm leaned in and whispered in his ear, following up with a playful nip and lick. "Anything you want, baby. I wish for oysters on the half-shell, caviar, smoked salmon, and two butter poached lobsters. Make it snappy and have them up in my room."

"But Master, we need--"

"Not now!" Randy glared at Karim. "Can't you see I have special guests? C'mon girls, see those stairs over here? Let's go up to my room. It's the biggest in the house and I promise you won't be disappointed."

Randy nudged the girls forward with playful pats against their bottoms. They giggled and hurried forward on their thin heels. The lone brunette of the quartet flashed Kim a smile, waggled her fingers, and then blew a kiss.

Blue and red lights flashed through the window and the squeal of tires was heard from the front drive. A moment later a loud knock pounded against the door. Randy shot a scowl over his shoulder, halfway up the stairs.

"Get that already, would you? Girls, go up. Last door on the left."

Karim sighed, moved into the living room doorway, and snapped his fingers. The front door opened on its own, admitting their mystery guest. Footsteps down the marble hall heralded his arrival. Karim bowed his head and gestured the man into the lavish room.

"You!" Randy's outraged voice filled the room. "I should have known when I saw those damn police lights. How dare you come here and spoil my fun, *Detective*." The way he sneered the last word made it an insult.

Rick Connor took a moment to assess the room, from the brief glimpse of the four girls disappearing up the stairs to Kimberly's tear stained face. Surprise registered on his face when he recognized her.

"Forgive the intrusion," Rick began. "However, this isn't a social visit. I need to ask you a few questions regarding yesterday's incident."

"This isn't a good time," Randy snapped. "And I have nothing to say to you, so get out."

Rick's expression hardened and he crossed his arms over his chest. "We can either do this the easy way or I can haul you down to the police station. I'm sure you recall what a lengthy process that can be. Your choice, Randy." Deep down, part of him seemed to wish that Randy would resist and give him enough trouble to make good on his threat. His brother deserved to be behind bars before he messed up and hurt somebody else. The way he'd hurt their family.

"Just make it quick, I'm busy." Randy stormed down the steps, brushed past Karim, and then flopped down on the second couch. Across from him, Kimberly scooted a little closer to Tamujin. Randy smirked at the unlikely pair.

"Looks like you're learning." Rick almost looked disappointed. "Slowly, but learning."

"Yeah, whatever, just get on with it and stop your gloating."

"All right. Where were--"

"I can't do it anymore!" Issa breezed into the room with Clip on her shoulder. Her body quivered and her eyes sparked brightly with anger, contrasting with the dark smudges beneath them. "I haven't slept."

"Or eaten!" Clip squawked. "Work, work, work, and no food. No rest."

Randy jumped up, arm snapping out and finger pointed toward the door. "Get back to the office. Now."

"No," Issa argued. "I won't do it and you can't treat me like this."

"Damn straight I can. I own you. All of you. You'll damn well do what I say. Get back in the office and take that feathered annoyance with you."

"What is going on here?" Rick's voice cut in. He stood up and looked between Issa and his brother. The two were staring each other down, neither one showing any sign of giving in. "Miss Issa, are you okay?"

Issa's gaze snapped to the side and she blinked, seeming only now to notice Rick's presence in the room. The fury faded from her face, which made her exhaustion all the more apparent. Despite that, she smiled.

"Inspector Connor?"

"Just call me Rick," he replied. He flashed her a brief, albeit no less jovial grin. Reluctantly, Rick took his eyes away from Issa and turned to Randy. His face hardened with disgust. "What are you doing to these people?"

"They're not people. They're genies," Randy spat back at him. "You don't even have any business in my house, so don't come here to judge me."

"We are not even 'people'. Did I hear that correctly?"

"You're a genie, Issa?" Rick asked. Duty and his feelings for Issa wavered, clashing against one another. On one hand, she was a beautiful and sweet young woman, and on the other hand, she was the source of the problem. He gritted his teeth and turned from Issa to Randy. "So you are the cause of the chaos in town."

"What chaos?" Randy asked.

"It's mad out there, total confusion. People are going crazy. Law and order went down the drain... And you're in here in your fancy mansion living up the life while our citizens die. What kind of person are you?"

"I just give people what they want. Is that so bad?" Randy asked. He shrugged, nonchalant about the whole matter. It was to the point outside that they were only a few steps away from someone calling Martial Law and taking over the city to restore order. The police couldn't handle it alone.

"Don't you know what's happening?" Rick asked.

"I haven't been on the streets for a while," Randy replied. He shrugged again.

Rick shook his head. His brother had always been an idiot and this only proved it. "You don't know the things I've seen out there, Randy. This city is falling apart and it's not going to last. People are getting hurt."

"Yeah? Tell me what's so bad."

"People are racing cars down Santa Monica Boulevard during rush hour. There's been three pileups since the day began. Two people died. One of them was a pregnant woman. The other a father of four."

"Accidents happen," Randy said.

"I saw a guy in an Indiana Jones outfit running down the street with a boulder rolling after him. People had to dive for cover to avoid it, but someone's kid has a broken leg now because of it. It stopped in a bakery shop window. That store's been there for over a decade and now it's trashed."

"They have insurance. It'll get replaced," Randy said again, shrugging his shoulders in the usual nonchalant way. "I did them a favor. Nobody needs baked goods these days anyway. They're fattening."

Randy, ever the smug jerk, had an excuse for every problem.

"There's people playing out old western movies on Rodeo Drive. They're on horses shooting at each other. There's kids walking tigers and elephants on leashes, but someone's tiger already ate a little girl's toy poodle."

"Good. Those little yappy dogs are noisy. She can get a real dog now like a German Shepherd."

The genies made disgusted sounds each time Randy discredited his brother's observations. The world was falling into chaos, and for as long as Randy owned their vessels, there was nothing they could do to stop it. Men sat in front of TVs drinking gallons of beer and eating mountains of food, destroying their livers and their hearts.

In the Latin quarter, everyone drove a Mercedes, BMW, Lamborghinis and other expensive cars. At night, no one could sleep due to the bass of their music systems. People fought and got into shoot outs over the tiniest scratch to their paintjobs.

Housewives no longer did their housework. They sat around beside their pools while drinking champagne. Some soaked in jacuzzis as manservants serviced their every need, relaxing away each day as their working husbands went to the office.

An ongoing battle raged in one residential community between two neighbors. Each one sat outside with their cordless phone and continuously tried to outdo the other. One wished for a boat and the other wish for a bigger boat. One wished for his house to become a villa and the other wished his into a medieval castle. It went on and on until their wishes resulted in utter chaos.

"I'm providing a public service," Randy spread his arms out wide and grinned. "People are getting everything they want and it's all thanks to me."

Rick shook his head. "People may be getting what they want, but they're not happy. They're addicted, always wanting more. This wish line of yours is like crack."

Randy's grin widened into Cheshire proportions. "It's great, isn't it? They'll keep coming for more. I'll be in business forever."

"Will you? How can you stay in business when no one has money anymore, huh? Nobody works anymore, Randy. Businesses are closed and schools are let out. Doctors, lawyers, shrinks... hell, even Jenny Craig is folding.

No jobs means no money." Rick stepped forward. "Families are falling apart. All people do is have orgies. It's all your fault."

"Maybe you need to go join one, Rick. This is fun."

Rick stared hard at his brother, derision etched into his features. "I will make this stop, Randy. I have to."

"I'll help you," Issa declared, moving closer to the officer. Clip flew to her shoulder.

"Me too, but on one condition," the parrot said. "I want regular, nutritious meals three times a day. At the least. No making me work through meal hours."

"You can't work for him," Randy spat out. "I own you both and you'll be staying right here, you ungrateful--"

"Enough!" Tamujin roared, cutting Randy off and silencing everyone. "We have no time for this, not when Gengir Xul has kidnapped Miss Byron's son. And we know where he is."

"Wait, what?" Rick turned to face Kimberly. "He's been kidnapped? Are you sure?"

"Yes," Kim cried. "That awful man has my baby."

"How do you know?" the bewildered cop asked.

Karim bowed his head. "We have means. Gengir Xul has her child and he will not give him up without a fight."

Rick scrubbed his hands down his face, his gaze travelling from each person in the room to the next. "All right, this is what's going to happen. I'm taking you all down to the station and we're going to get to the bottom of this."

"Impossible," Tamujin argued. He tightened his grip around Kim's shoulders. "My family and I must remain in a protected area, or we risk bringing Gengir Xul down upon us."

"The precinct is perfectly safe."

"No." Karim shook his head. "We saw on the news what happened the last time you held Gengir Xul in your prison. He will find us, claim us, and, if we are lucky, kill us."

Issa's soft whimper drew Rick's gaze. He studied her pale face and frightened golden eyes. "If that's the case, then you all stay here," he said. "I'll take Randy in."

"What? You bastard!" Randy stomped toward his brother and pointed a finger in his face. "I have people upstairs waiting for me. Beautiful people. I'm not leaving them here."

"Well if you'd like, I can bring them in too. I'm sure they don't have any reason to be worried about seeing the police, right?" Rick didn't blink as he held Randy's gaze. His brother's face reddened.

"Fine, whatever," Randy grumbled. "They can wait here."

"Do not worry, Master." Karim grinned and bowed his head. "I will keep them entertained."

The look Randy shot at the genie was less than thrilled.

"The story of my life," he complained, crossing toward the door with Rick. "Someone else always gets the cream."

Chapter 15

By the dim light of the moon, Gengir Xul examined the shimmering dome encapsulating the quiet, ostentatious mansion. Magic sparked and crackled, visible only to his arcane sight. The men behind him remained oblivious to the mystical barrier that kept him out. Their greedy eyes were focused on the house, their thoughts on the loot they'd be able to snatch in this raid.

Fools. All they see is the wealth and not the true power available within. He'd let them have their petty treasures and money. All he wanted were the genies. *His* genies.

"What's the plan, Boss?" Crush rubbed his hands together.

"Lead your men inside and bring me as many of them as you can. Trash the place when you're done."

"Not a problem, Boss. We got this."

Crush raised his arm in the air and beckoned his gang forward. They stormed across the lawn and smashed their way into the mansion through the windows. Crush led the way through the darkened hallways, directing his guys to move through each room. He moved up the stairs, saw light shining from beneath a doorway, and then kicked the door in.

Screams filled the room and Crush leered at the four naked women in the bed. The man lying in the middle of the tangle leapt up with a startled cry.

"You are not welcome here! Leave!"

"Nah, I think this here gun says I get to stay and have some fun." Crush brandished his weapon then pointed it at the fuming genie. The man moved his hands through the air, tracing a magical glyph, and vanished.

"Well one's a loss, but now I get the four of you. Wrap them up for the boss, boys. It's chilly outside." Crush grinned and raked his eyes down the girls.

"Hey, we didn't get paid for this!" the brunette cried as she was yanked from the bed.

Crush ignored her and left the room, moving farther down the hall. He found Issa in the next bedroom, his grin widening when he recognized her.

"Wakey, wakey little girl."

Issa's silky hair bunched in his grip as he took a handful and gave a jerk. Her eyes flew open and she swung her fists in a blind attack, but Crush was ready for it and grabbed her wrists in his other hand.

"Now sweetheart, that ain't any way to greet a friend, is it? Looks like you and me are gonna get to have some fun after all."

Despite her struggles, Crush dragged Issa out into the hall where he met another of his men who had Aboo slung over his shoulder.

"What do you want us to do now? The others disappeared, but I snagged this one before he could get away."

"Burn it," Crush ordered. "Tell the boys they have two minutes to snag whatever loot they want, then to light the rooms on fire."

The gangsters became kidnappers as they crossed the yard with their captives. Gengir Xul looked upon them with disapproval and shook his head. This wasn't what he'd sent them for. He'd asked them for seven genies, but his accomplices returned with loose women and prostitutes. He growled.

"What am I going to do with the hookers?" he demanded, his loud voice booming loudly across the yard. A couple of the thugs grimaced and shrank back a few steps as if his voice could do them harm. For all they knew, it could.

"You said everybody, boss," Crush answered reluctantly.

The heel of the sorcerer's palm connected with Crush's face with enough force to swing the gangbanger around on his feet. His fellow thugs looked on in silence, and none dared to speak afterward either.

***

After an entire night at the police department, an exhausted Randy returned to his mansion to find fire trucks blocking the driveway. The manor was empty and the genies were gone.

"What the hell...?" he wondered out loud.

The charred walls of the mansion barely stood, holding empty window frames with shattered fragments of glass remaining. His home looked like a war zone in the Middle East.

As he stepped from the car to approach the home, a police officer stopped him.

"Excuse me, sir. You'll have to stay back."

"But that's my house," Randy yelled.

"I'm sorry, sir. I hope you have good insurance," the officer said, as if that consolation would in any way lighten Randy's spirits.

This is awful, Randy thought. *It's a good thing that I have genies to fix this. Whatever the hell happened, my house can be as good as new by tomorrow at least.* "I've got something better," Randy said mysteriously.

"Huh?" the officer asked.

By morning, the last of the fire had been extinguished and law enforcement were on their way from the area. Randy waited until they were gone before he ran inside to view the destruction. They'd strictly told him to stay out and that it wasn't safe, but he knew better. The genies had to be inside.

The interior of the mansion was a smoldering ruin that presented a complete view of the overall damage. From the blackened walls to the ash-covered furnishings, little appeared to be salvageable. The genies had to have been hiding while the fire raged, but he knew they were back inside now. They had to be.

How could they sit by and let his house burn? Anger broiled through Randy as he stormed through the damaged hallways and deeper into the heart of the mansion. He followed the sound of raised voices.

Karim and Tamujin's loud shouts allowed Randy to follow the argument to their location. Salima sat nearby at the bottom of the stairs with Clip on her lap. His singed feathers appeared beyond repair, blackened at their tips. Randy wondered if the fire happened when someone had tried to roast the bird, and decided he couldn't blame them if they did. His loud cries and constant need to eat had tempted Randy into nearly shoving him into an oven too.

"Shh... it's all right," Salima soothed him. She alternated between feeding him crackers and running her fingers over his remaining feathers.

Abdul walked back and forth across the blackened room, his gaze focused on a crystal ball. The magical orb floated in mid-air, moving with him in his frantic pacing.

"What the hell do you think you're doing?" Randy strode over and grabbed Abdul by his bony shoulders. The crystal ball dropped to the ground and shattered into a million glittering pieces. "You all let this happen! Look at my house!"

Rough hands tipped in sharp claws jerked Randy away from Abdul. Tamujin opened his fanged mouth and roared in Randy's face, ready to bite the man's face off. Terrified, Randy squeaked like a mouse and trembled in the large genie's grip.

"No, Tamujin, wait!" Karim cried.

"Why? This one has caused us nothing but trouble and pain."

"We need him," Abdul interjected. "He is our Master."

"And without him we cannot do anything," Karim finished. "Please, Tamujin. I understand your anger, but now is not the time."

With a final low, warning growl, Tamujin released his human master and pushed him away. Randy stumbled back and glared at all of the genies.

"Right. Now that that's over, tell me this. What. The. Hell. Happened?"

"Gengir Xul, happened," Salima said, bitterness in her voice.

"You lot said that forcefield you put up would keep him out." Randy crossed his arms over his chest.

"He sent in his allies," Abdul clarified. "The barrier did not keep them out and they took both Aboo and Issa. We must get them back before he takes them to Demon Land."

"No, I don't think so." Randy shook his head. "Two genies more, two genies less, what difference does it make?"

The others froze and stared at him with varying degrees of shock and disgust on their faces.

"They are family," Karim stressed. "Didn't you ever have a family?"

"No, not really."

"Figures," Clip said balefully.

"But, your brother..." Karim prodded.

Randy sneered at him. "Is no brother to me."

As if their talk summoned him, Rick stepped through the charred ruins with Kimberly at his side. They picked their way through the mess carefully until they reached the disgruntled group. Tamujin pulled Kim close and comforted her at his side.

"Your home," Kim cried a she cast a dismayed glance around the place.

"Where are the rest of you?" Rick looked over the group. "Where's Issa? And the kid?"

"Gone," Karim replied. The genie kicked at a soggy piece of furniture.

"Gone where?" Rick asked, pressing for further information.

Salima sighed and rose from her seat. "Kidnapped, she and Aboo both, by Gengir Xul's men."

"That's who took my Luke."

"All right, I'm placing you all under police protection," Rick said, only to be swiftly interrupted by a snort from Randy. "Something you wanna say?"

Randy straightened his shoulders and sneered up at his brother. "Yeah, I do. I know all about your so called 'protection' and I'm not buying it. You can count me the hell out. And you can forget about taking *my* genies as well."

"Too bad." Rick lifted his radio, ready to call for reinforcements.

"Wait!" Abdul jumped between the two men. "Please, wait you do not know what you are up against."

"He's right," Karim agreed. "We must work together. Besides, we can tell you where Gengir Xul is holding Issa, Aboo, and Luke."

Uncertainty rippled across Rick's face, but he lowered his radio without activating it. "You can? How?"

"With this." Karim drew the magic mirror out of his vest and gestured for everyone to gather round. He swept his slender fingers over the glass, murmured a quiet incantation, and summoned up a vision in the mystical glass.

Chapter 16

Thickets of tall weeds and unclipped grass littered the back yard to the rear of the warehouse. Once the gang members cleared the ground and made space, Gengir Xul drew a large pentagram in the newly created space, using a piece of a child's sidewalk chalk. One of the gang members must have nabbed it from his own child perhaps, in a bid to gain favor with their new boss.

They were petrified, but it was out of their control now. They'd reached the point of no return when their former leader perished during the scuffle with the cops and Gengir, the demon, saved them from incarceration. They'd all be in jail now if not for him.

He was evil. He had to be evil, and without anyone to stop him, they were forced to do his bidding until the very end. In fear of their lives, they served and worked with desperate zeal to provide his every wish, hoping against hope that once he regained control of his genies, he allowed them the freedom to leave.

Or better yet, maybe he'd make kings of them all for their loyal service. Some of the gang members weren't terrified of their new boss. They worshipped him, eager to please and equally eager to receive the crumbs of his success. Eagerly rubbing their hands together, they spectated from the sidelines as he called the demons forth. They didn't care about the three kids in the circle; money and fame became their true desires.

Issa, Aboo, and Luke remained helpless, confined to a fate as tokens for the demon lord Shabalis.

In a flourish, Gengir whipped a magic wand from his cloak and aimed it toward the sky. He drew a five-pointed star in the air while chanting incantations in a guttural voice. The clouds, dark as pitch against the eerie night, revealed no stars until the glowing red pentagram appeared. With its creation, a vortex formed to disperse the clouds. The winds swirled hard and sharp, twisting around the sorcerer and his captives.

It was the beginning of the end and with the genies as his gift to the demon, all would become right in his world. He chuckled darkly at the end of his spell.

"Shabalis, my Master, come, come!"

The central point of the swirling mist emitted a crimson light. Within moments, the horrifying face of the Archdemon Shabalis appeared within. It glowered out over the crowd and made some of the gangster quake with absolute fear. Even for those who had willingly served Gengir out of greed, the sight proved to be more than they anticipated. Regret, terror, and disbelief ruled the night. What they had done was no better than making a deal with the devil, and maybe, just maybe they had.

"I thought you'd never call. What have we here?"

Issa embraced the boys protectively, like a mother over her hens. She crouched above them and hid their faces against her blouse. Fearing the apparition, neither risked looking upon Shabalis' disturbing visage.

"Two genies and a human hostage," Gengir Xul replied with triumph.

"Only two? You're losing your touch, Gengir Xul."

"It's not my fault. They have prisons, and trucks, and contracts, and 900 nurnbers... It's a different world now..."

Shabalis snorted derisively, accepting no excuses. His unimpressed, gleaming red eyes stared through the souls of the onlookers. It seared them like flames and left one gangster trembling in fear.

"Excuses, excuses. You need debriefing. I'm taking you all to Demon Land."

"Good. I need a vacation," Gengir Xul replied.

Without warning, the spinning circle of clouds corkscrewed downward like a twister, descending so sharply several of the gang members screamed. Some shrieked and broke ranks to flee for their lives while others stared, frozen by their terror. It engulfed the sorcerer and his prisoners, leaving only the diabolic circle behind. And even then, no one dared to touch it, fearing they too would suffer the very same fate.

***

At the mansion, the group of genies, Randy, Rick, and Kimberly broke the circle. Kim staggered back with tears streaming down her face. Her poor Luke had been petrified and she hadn't been there to save him. In all of her life as a mother, she'd never felt as much a failure as she did now. She hadn't protected him when he needed her most and now he was in... Demon Land. It sounded like Hell.

"Oh, God! I'll never see my little boy again!" she wept into her hands.

"You will!" Tamujin declared.

Kimberly lifted her tear-soaked face to him. His fierce features should have startled and scared her again, but she took an odd comfort in the emotion that he displayed. She wanted to believe in him.

"The time has come to make a move," Abdul said. "Issa and Aboo need us; Tanju, the magic stone, needs our intervention. We cannot delay any longer without facing the repercussions. Tanju is dying."

Rick, confused by the unfamiliar situation, made up his own mind. If demons had a tangible form to harm and kidnap others, then that meant they could be harmed as well. In his cop brain, he formed a dangerous logic and determined there could be no alternative. Grimly, he glanced from Kim to the other genies. "We have to bring them back. I'll take my men and..."

"It won't work that way," Tamujin interrupted.

"He thinks he's Dirty Harry or some sort of bloody hero. Let him go if he wants. No skin off my back."

The genies all turned their heads toward Randy and fixed him with their unwavering gazes.

"What?" Randy asked. "Why is everyone giving me the stink-eye?"

"Because *you* are the one who has to go," Abdul replied in his serious tone.

"Me? Why me?"

Karim stepped forward and provided the answer Randy dreaded. "Because you are the only one who can pass through the Gate of Ganzir. You have done so before and now you must do so again."

"No way!" Randy argued, stepping back. "I'm not going anywhere."

"Kids are missing, Randy. You are going to go." Rick closed the space between himself and his brother. "And I'm going with you."

"Ha!" Randy scoffed. "You and me together on the same side, Rick? You must be kidding."

"The officer puts forth a good plan. Count me in," Tamujin said, his feral grin making Randy take a small step backward.

"And me, too," Clip declared from Karim's shoulder. "Anything to get Issa and Aboo back."

"Well you can go without me," Randy spat, glaring at them all in turn. "I won't do it. No way."

Rick scowled, irritation written plain across his features with no attempt to hide it away. "Do you remember that time I caught you working with the Colombians, crap loads of dope in your apartment? You were dealing and I let you go because you were my brother."

"Are you still hanging on about that? Will you ever let me forget it? Let it go already, Rick."

"Let it go? Do you know how long I can put you away behind bars for dealing drugs in that quantity? Ten, maybe fifteen years. I still have the records, Randy."

"That's fucking blackmail!" Randy roared, incensed.

"Yeah, well, that seems to be the only language you understand."

The two brothers glared at one another in a silent standoff for several moments. Red blotches stood out on Randy's face while Rick remained cool as a cucumber in the face of his brother's anger.

"Goddammit, fine. As if I have a choice in the matter."

"Finally, that's settled." Clip clacked his beak and mantled his wings before settling back down. "But how can the rest of us pass through the Gate?"

Abdul supplied an answer no one wanted to hear. "Randy is our master. He can wish you to be a demon."

"What? Oh no!" Clip hopped up in the air and made an agitated circuit around the room, knocking a framed award certificate from the wall. He resettled on Tamujin's broad shoulders.

"Only for a short time," Salima reassured the parrot.

"What about me? What am I supposed to do against demons?" Randy raised a brow, certain he was going to regret helping.

"We will arm you as best we can." Rubbing his chin in thought, Karim stepped forward and looked Randy over from head to toe. "I can supply demon catchers, spirit shields, and devil blasters. The works. You will be fine, Master."

"Oh. Great. I'm so reassured." No one missed the sarcasm in his tone but neither did they remark on it.

"You are our only hope, Master Randy. Please. We would not send you in unprotected."

"Whatever you say. So," Randy said, clapping his hands together, "let's go get this done then. Off to Demon Land. Just make sure to pick me up a t-shirt on the way out."

Chapter 17

The mood was somber in the mansion as the group prepared for their foray into the dreaded world of dark sorcery and evil. Demon Land's name might have been reminiscent of an amusement park, but it was the furthest thing from a happy and fun place anyone could ever find.

As promised, Karim procured several magical items to arm the chosen team with. He passed over bracelets made from braided gold, silver, and iron to Randy and Rick.

"Spirit shields, as promised. These should ward off the worst effects of Demon Land's dark aura."

Behind the trio, Clip pecked at a food filled tray, gobbling down juicy peaches, sweet dates, and sticky honeyed pastries.

"You'll make yourself sick, eating so fast." Salima frowned at the pulpy mess Clip left on the table. "Slow down."

"I wish I could take this all with me. Who knows how long it'll take down there. I could starve. Wither away."

The elder genie sighed at Clip's dramatics and shook her head. Rather than chastise him again for his piggish behavior, she smoothed her hand over his feathered back. "Worry not, Clip. Master will provide for you, you have only to ask."

"Him? Are you kidding? He doesn't even want to go. You think he's going to give me cookies for making him?"

Ignoring Clip's usual feeding frenzy, Tamujin crept closer to Kimberly and wrapped his muscled arm around her quaking shoulders.

"I will find your Luke," he consoled. "I promise you this, Kimberly."

Faint mascara tracks smudged Kim's eyes and cheeks, most of her makeup washed away in her earlier sobs. She looked up at Tamujin, lower lip trembling and eyes glistening with tears.

"Are you doing this for me?" she asked in a whisper.

"I cannot bear to see you cry." With his thumb he wiped away a single teardrop from her cheek, infinitely gentle in his touch. His kindness set off the full waterworks and Kimberly threw herself into his embrace, hugging him tight.

"Please be careful, Tam. I don't... I don't want to lose you, too!"

Abdul glanced over the different little groups, face grim. "It is time," he announced to the room. "We cannot delay further. Every moment we waste is another moment for their power to grow."

Salima joined Abdul's side. Both turned and faced Randy, motioning for Clip, Rick, and Tamujin to join him in the center of the living room.

"Please, Master, you must make the wish and we will send you on your way," Salima bid him.

"I wish... I..." Randy looked around the room, a touch of green in his pale pallor. "You know what, I don't wish."

"Randy!" Rick barked.

"Fine! I wish to stand at the Gate of Ganzir with my no-good brother, the beastly one, and the cranky bird. God I can't believe I'm saying that."

The world around the small group twisted, multiple colors swirling into a dizzying vortex. Their stomachs flipped, their ears popped, and in less than five heartbeats they stood in a dim chamber rather than the opulent mansion.

"Ugh, I feel sick," Randy wheezed. Rick appeared as green as his brother even though he kept his complaints silent.

"You get used to it," Clip shared.

In the semi-darkness they could make out little more than rock and a narrow tunnel, but Randy recognized the architecture of the gate. It appeared the same as the first one he had encountered. The one that had led him into this whole mess to begin with.

"May we have some light please?"

"As you wish," a deep voice intoned from the darkness. The bass sound rumbled through them, rattling their teeth. A soft glow emanated from the stone around them and gradually grew in brightness.

"What is this place?" Rick swiveled his head around, trying to take in every nook and cranny of the subterranean cavern. His eyes widened as he took in the ancient gate. Blackened bars kept them from moving forward through the passage. Arcane sigils decorated every square inch of the stone frame, sometimes seeming to glow red then deep purple.

"The entrance to hell," Randy answered, smirking. "I'm glad I can take you back home."

Randy aimed a frown toward his brother. "Hell or not, at least I came willingly."

"You're only here because it's your job," Randy snarled back.

"I came because it's the ri--"

The deep, disembodied voice interrupted them. "Are you entering or not? I haven't got all eternity."

"What's the matter with you?" Randy snapped at the gate. "You having a crappy day, too?"

"All my days are bad," the unseen Guardian sighed.

"Yeah, well welcome to the club, bub."

"Master!" Tamujn hissed, horrified by Randy's disrespectful tone.

Randy waved the big genie off and continued to address the gate guardian. "Look, since we don't want to keep you waiting and ruin your day further, are you going to let us in or what?"

"The soulless one may enter. The rest must remain without."

On Tamujin's shoulder, Clip shifted from foot to foot and ruffled his blue feathers. "Here comes the tough part."

"You must now turn us into demons, Master, so the rest of us may pass," the fanged genie directed.

A devilish gleam entered Randy's eyes and his grin stretched to Grinch-like proportions as he turned toward his brother. "Oh, it'll be my pleasure. I wish--"

"Wait!" Clip squawked. "Wait!"

"What now?" The bird received an irritated look.

"The spirit shields Karim made. We can put them on and try that first. Maybe it'll work."

"I have them right here." Rick pulled the bracelets from his pocket and passed one over to Tamujin. He fastened a second around Clip's neck, and then the third around his own wrist.

"Hey, what about me?"

"You have no soul, Master," Tamujin stated straight out. "You lost it a long time ago. Therefore, you have no need of a spirit shield."

"Time is ticking..." the Guardian droned.

"Do you talk to your master like this?" Randy had almost had it with the bossy Guardian. He hated to be rushed on things.

"All the time. Now, in or out? We're closing in five minutes."

"Nothing worse than a crank doorman," Randy muttered under his breath.

"Four minutes."

"You know, if you ever consider a career change you'd make a great bouncer."

"Don't piss him off!" Clip cried in alarm.

The Guardian ignored Randy's flippant tone and instead asked, "What's a bouncer?"

"Never mind then."

"Three minutes."

"We're coming already. Sheesh." Randy beckoned the others and stepped toward the gateway. The black bars vanished, leaving the way open for them all to step through.

"All that hustle and not even a tip," The Guardian sighed. "I hate this job."

"Here's a tip for ya," Randy called over his shoulder. "Find a better day job."

"Seriously, Randy, do you have to be an ass to everyone you come across?" Rick admonished him, frowning.

"Do you have to be such a goody--"

The passage ahead grew dark and the floor beneath their feet fell away. The group's startled cries filled the air as they tumbled through the pitch black emptiness. They hit the ground in a pile, the loose grit and scratchy sand doing little to cushion their fall.

"Ugh, where are we?"

Where before as they fell there had been darkness, now there was light. Torches illuminated an endless passage bordered on either side by tall, sheer cliff walls. Multiple doorways and windows were carved into the walls at varying levels and the occasional archway branched across over their heads.

"Demon Land," Tamujin whispered, the first hints of fear in his voice.

Deep, rumbling growls and piercing screeches bounced back and forth between the rocky walls. The cacophony of sound assaulted their ears, inspiring fear and doubt. A passing shadow pulled their gazed upward, where a large winged demon flew across the chasm. Something dark lingered in a high window, chittering curses after the flying monstrosity, and then a foul stream of water sloshed down over the group. The putrid liquid soaked into their hair and clothes, and gummed up Clip's wings.

"Great. Just great." Randy wiped the dirty stuff from his face. "We landed in a demon slum of all places."

"It could be worse," Tamujin helped everyone to their feet.

"Yeah? How's that?" Randy couldn't believe anything was worse than devil piss.

"We could have arrived in their torture rooms," the genie answered. His words made everyone pale.

"Then we probably shouldn't linger around." Rick gathered his wits first and tried to get them back on track. "How do we find our way around here? And where will we find the others?"

"Maybe you should knock and ask for directions."

"Look, Randy, we all know you don't want to be here, but drop the act. You started this so for once, be a man and own up to it."

Rick's chastisement did the trick. Randy scowled but said nothing.

"There is a way," Tamujin offered when the fight seemed to be over. "Genie magic gets warped and distorted here, so I brought a pendulum with me."

Tamujin pulled a silver chain from his pocket. At the end of the delicate links hung a polished crystal point.

"Err, not to sound dumb but... A pendulum?" Rick skepticism was echoed by Randy. It was their first agreement.

"Yes. When everything else fails, there is always a pendulum to guide your way. It is primitive, I admit, but you'll find nothing more reliable."

Glass shattered somewhere ahead and above them, followed by more screeches. The sounds were worse than nails on a chalkboard, sending chills down their spines and raising the hairs on their necks.

"We better get the hell out of here before they spot us and realize we don't belong," Randy said. He glanced back over his shoulder in time to see a humped shape slither across the passageway.

"Agreed." Rick motioned for Tamujin to lead the way.

Suspended from the chain, the pendulum winked and shined in the darkness. It swung back and forth, the crystal point spinning around in a circle. Finally, it stabilized, and pointed them forward.

Sticking close together, they moved down the narrow street. It didn't take long before Clip spotted a slinking figure following them. He cried out in alarm and pushed them to hurry forward.

The catlike demon sprang after them, wings snapping out from its brindled sides. It soared after them, maw opened wide and pointed fangs stained with old blood.

"Faster," Clip cried. "Faster! It's gaining on us."

"Can't you shoot it?"

Rick took his brother's idea to heart. He pulled his gun and aimed back toward the pursuing beast. The bullets bounced off its thick hide.

"Shoot it dead already!" Randy screamed.

"I'm *trying*!"

"This way!" Tamujin made a sharp left hand turn. The path narrowed further and the lighting grew dimmer, but they dared not slow. The demon chased after them, hot on their heels. Rick gave up on trying to shoot and focused on speeding his steps instead.

The path ahead seemed to open up and the group put on a bust of speed. By the time they saw the open chasm, it was too late to stop. They tumbled down into the darkness, cackling laughter following them down.

***

Terrifying visuals decorated the interior walls of the chamber, depicting images of desecration and murder. The macabre art lead to a long staircase, which rose to a throne flanked by candles burning in human skull holders. Drums and demonic laughter blended into an intimidating, noisy roar.

Shabalis sat on his throne with Gengir Xul hovering by his side. Issa sat on the floor at the foot of the throne, adorned in skimpy clothing and chained. Aboo and Luke were chained to each side.

"We can conquer their world easily," Gengir Xul said to his master. "We'll have millions, billions of souls at our command."

Shabalis stroked his chin and gazed thoughtfully at his three prisoners. They were toys to him, nothing more than cattle for his amusement to slay or torture on a whim. It didn't matter that they were children.

"That's a lot of soul-power," the demon lord muttered.

"Yes! We can change them all into demons. We can rule worlds, dimensions, universes. You name it, and it'll be ours."

"We?" Shabalis turned his head slowly toward Gengir Xul. A terrifying grin spread over his face, revealing teeth like razor sharpened pikes. "Ours, you say?"

"I mean... You, Master, with me by your side. When the stone dies, there will be nothing that can stop us."

In another chamber in the dungeons, the stone of power Tanju flickered faintly. They kept it contained within a stone post inscribed with sorcerous inscriptions. Like a living creature, Tanju fought for its life. Every so often, its irregular heartbeat echoed over the dungeon walls. It was dying and wouldn't last long.

"They're coming," Gengir Xul said suddenly, detecting an intrusion. "The humans are on their way, Master."

"I know they're coming. We'll soon have their souls in our grasp," Shabalis said.

Issa struggled against her bonds but was without the magic to overcome the chain's strength. "It won't be that easy. They will defeat you and rescue us."

"You'll be surprised. If you live that long, that is," Gengir Xul said. He chuckled and yanked her chain, dragging Issa off balance. She stumbled and fell as Aboo tried to catch her. Unfortunately, his chain was too short to reach her and she toppled to the hard ground.

"You'll pay for this," Aboo cried out, his voice shaking.

Booming laughter echoed through the room. Shabalis bent over in his throne, shoulders shaking with his amusement. "Do you hear that, Xul? The boy, he is actually threatening me."

"Insolent cur. You will soon decorate this dais, like all before you who were stupid enough to anger Lord Shabalis." Gengir Xul rested his hand on one of the many skull candleholders surrounding the throne.

"Yes, and it is high time we redecorated."

* * *

"Where are we this time?" Randy groaned and rolled onto his back. His body was sore, but as far as he could tell nothing was broken. "Clip? Tamujin? Rick?"

"I'm here, but I can't see a thing," Rick replied, somewhere to the right.

"Welcome to the heart of Demon Land." Tamujin's voice sounded from behind Randy. "Clip, are you well?"

"I-I-I'm scared," the bird answered. Randy reached out a hand slowly until his fingers brushed against feathers. Clip had sounded close and now that guess was confirmed. The parrot hopped onto his wrist and moved up his arm until he reached Randy's shoulder.

"Is everyone in one piece?" Rick asked.

"Yeah, I think so, but what's that noise?"

Everyone went quiet, but a dry rustling sounded from a few feet away. A soft thud followed, almost like a footstep.

"I wish there was some light in here," Randy muttered. In an instant, flames roared to life over the group. The fire licked at their clothes and singed their hair.

"No! Forget it! I take it back!" Randy screamed, prompting the fire to die immediately.

"Your wishes will not work here, Master," Tamujin explained. "You will always get something else than what you wish for. Similar, but different. Twisted, you might say. As we just learned, it can be catastrophic under the circumstances."

"You didn't think to mention that earlier?"

"We know now," Rick intervened before Randy's anger could swell to epic proportions. "No more wishes."

Unappeased, Randy grumbled under his breath. "We still need to see."

"Allow me."

A dim glow bloomed, slowly growing in strength. It took randy a moment to realize the light came from Tamujin's finger. He blinked, then snickered under his breath, reminded of a family friendly alien movie from his childhood.

Shaking off the absurd memory, Randy stood up and brushed off his pants. Less than three feet away the floor gave way into another abyss.

"We were lucky." Rick peered over the edge.

Randy disagreed. "It's hard to share your optimism."

"Near-death experiences always make me hungry," Clip muttered. "Can we—?"

"Not now!" Tamujin interrupted him sharply, much to Randy's immense relief. The bird brain constantly thought with his stomach and seemed incapable of remaining on task for long without something in his mouth. Randy rolled his eyes and watched Tamujin consult his pendulum. It swung in the direction of the chasm.

"Great! How the hell are we supposed to follow? Flying?" Randy asked.

Tamujin shook his head. "There may be another way."

"Where?" Randy asked.

Tamujin pointed his glowing finger. The faint light illuminated a narrow shaft stretching over the precipice like a bridge.

Randy stared at it, then whirled to face his companion. "No way! I'm afraid of heights. You couldn't pay me to cross that... well... maybe for money, but I'm not crossing it!"

Tamujin shook his head.

"We have no choice. It's the only way out. If we don't, we'll be forced to stay here forever."

Randy scoffed and glanced behind them, considering whether or not it was worth returning to the demon slum. When he turned, he saw a monstrous snake descending the rock wall and heading toward them from Demon Land.

"I change my mind. Let's go, I hate snakes."

"Why? You're closely related," Rick said.

Rick drew his gun and aimed it at the snake. It hissed and flicked its forked tongue, scenting them on the air. Randy's skin crawled as he recognized the meaning of the snake's slight sway and observant stare. It was measuring them, determining the best angle from which to attack and consume one of them. Randy shivered.

"Do something!"

"I don't really know what to do with snakes," Tamujin said.

"You're a damned genie!" Randy groaned into one hand. "Don't just stand there, Rick. Shoot it!"

Rick pulled the trigger and filled the snake with hot lead. At least, Randy imagined that would be the outcome until the slithering demon laughed. The hissing sound raised goosebumps on his arms and sent an icy trickle down his back.

Brilliant lightning arcs lanced outward from the serpent's mouth. The blue-white sparks sizzled against Rick's gun and knocked the weapon from his hands. It clattered over the stone ground and dropped over the precipice.

"Get moving!" Clip cried, alarm and terror in his voice.

Tamujin and Rick stepped onto the ledge while Randy lingered behind them. The precarious height gave him a legitimate reason to halt. Maybe he was a thief, but he'd never tolerated heights well and had an aversion to being a high distance off the ground. He was also too much of a man to admit he was scared.

"You can do it," Clip encouraged him. "Don't look down and you'll be okay."

Randy put his foot on the ledge and nearly lost his balance. He scurried back again, breathing hard and fast while his head swam.

"Every genie's nightmare, a wimpy master. Just my luck, I guess," Clip muttered.

"I'm not a coward," Randy argued.

An enormous, inhuman eye appeared in the stone wall behind them. It shifted until the vertical, slit pupil focused on the group. "Holy shit," Randy muttered as it narrowed to stare at them. Guttural laughter and the malevolent sound of drums resonated through the surrounding area. The shudder of a large earth quake showered Randy and clip with small stones and bits of debris. He didn't bother to dust off his shoulders; he ran as quickly as he could, forgetting his fear of heights. Clip followed and soon they caught up to Tamujin and Rick.

"I can see the other side," Tamujin said to him.

A horrific structure, resembling a palace from a bad dream, loomed on the edge of the precipice. An ominous shaft led straight into its gaping entrance, the most terrifying thing Randy had ever seen that wasn't a prison shower room. He shuddered and stopped in his tracks. The quick halt made him lose balance, but as his arms waved and he came close to toppling into the chasm, Rick reached out to catch him. Randy dangled dangerously close to toppling in, suspended by his arms while his brother struggled to pull him up.

"You... you should lose some weight," Rick grunted out. He breathed hard with exertion, every inch gained nothing less than a fight.

"I'll see Jenny Craig. If we live through this."

"Do that."

With help from Tamujin, Rick managed to pull Randy onto the bridge.

"They're coming!" Clip cried.

A swarm of demons flew toward them from the direction of the demon slum. The sound of many wings filled the air, their leathery, membranous flaps making loud whoosh sounds as they approached. The trio had no choice but to turn and run as monsters pursued them from the demon slum. The gate to the palace was still too far.

"We won't make it!" Randy exclaimed.

"Here, try these, Master!"

Tamujin removed talismans resembling Native American dream catchers from his robes and distributed them to his companions. The web interlacing the circle twisted in a spiral, containing a black stone in the middle.

"How could this help us?" Randy asked.

"You'll see. It works like magic."

Duh, Randy thought. *It is magic, you idiot.* He didn't argue or voice his thoughts out loud and merely tried to look grateful instead.

The horde of demons was upon them. Demonic eyes glowed like embers in the semi-darkness, illuminating their bestial faces and glistening on the saliva dripping from their curved fangs. Long talons reached out to catch their prey.

Tamujin extended the demon catcher before him. Randy and Rick copied him.

The demonic entities quickly skidded to a stop, but momentum carried them forward. The panic showed on their inhuman, terrified faces. Even the flying monsters attempted to swerve and change directions, but they had been speeding too fast to bank sharply to either direction.

Despite Randy's doubt, the dream catcher worked in a snap. The closest two demons fell into the trap and were caught by the web, flailing and unable to escape as they shrank and were inevitably swallowed into the central stone. They shrieked the entire time.

"There!" Tamujin shouted victoriously.

"Where is clip?" Randy asked.

"Uh oh," Rick said. He pointed with one hand toward the rest of the demons who escaped. They disappeared into the entrance of the palace and one of them held a struggling Clip in its talons.

***

Tanju dimmed, its beating pulse slowing. The sluggish beat was weak and barely holding on.

"It is almost done." Shabalis grinned and held his hand over the dying stone.

"Indeed. Then power will be yours, Lord." Gengir Xul held out Clip's limp body. "What shall I do with this little skinny thing?"

Shabalis gave Clip little more than a passing glance. "Make me some parrot soup," he suggested. "I hear it tastes delicious."

"Sadly, I never learned how to cook."

"Pity." Shabalis sighed and waved Gengir Xul away. "Toss him with the others."

"With pleasure."

A deep bow preceded Gengir Xul's departure from the chamber. His heavy footsteps echoed down the stone hallway, sending various imps and small demon scurrying from his path. He followed the twisting corridor until he came upon a low well.

"Let's see how your friends are doing," Gengir Xul laughed, peering down the deep pit. A nearby rat overreached for a fat bug and tumbled over the edge. Far below, Issa shrieked as the rodent struck her head.

The three young prisoners clung to the walls of the pit, using whatever small nooks and crannies they could find to maintain their footing. Their pale faces peered up at Gengir Xul and he leered down at them.

"Enjoying your time with Lord Shabalis' pet?" Far below, in the pit's bottom, a lame dragon paced in a tight circle, expelling gouts of flame every few minutes. "Stormfist gets cranky when he's not fed. You really should do yourselves a favor and give up trying to get away. It'll go better for you that way. Faster. Maybe even less painful."

"When I get out of here, I'm going to... to..." Aboo blustered.

"You're going to what?" Gengir Xul laughed.

"You'll pay for this," Issa hissed when Aboo didn't speak up.

"I'm sure I will, but for now... Here, Storm Fist, have an appetizer. Tastes like chicken. I'm sure you'll love it." He tossed Clip's unconscious body down the pit and left them to their prison.

"Clip!" Aboo cried out in alarm as the feathered body plummeted downward. Below them, the eager dragon reared up on its hind legs and opened its massive jaws.

Issa reached out and tried to catch him, but her fingers barely brushed against his feathers. Aboo and Luke fared no better. Just when it seemed Clip was dragon chow, he flapped his wings weakly and swooped out of range from the snapping fangs.

Fly, Clip, fly!" Luke encourages, his words reciprocated by a cheering Aboo and Issa.

Clip reached as high as Issa's shoulders and took a perch. The sharp dig of his talons drew a thin trickle of blood.

"Gently, little brother, gently!"

"I... almost... became... dragon food," the quaking parrot heaved.

"But you didn't. You're safe now, but only so long as I can keep my grip and I can't do that if you bleed me dry."

"Sorry." He loosened his tight hold. "Now what? I don't want to be a dragon snack."

"Everybody needs to eat," the dragon spoke up, startling them all.

"You talk?" Luke's voice squeaked up an octave. Issa admired the human boy's bravery so far.

"All I have to say is I am hungry." Once again the scaled beast snapped its jaws and tried to reach them.

"You know," Clip called down, "I'm hungry too, but you have to watch your diet. Eat what's good for you."

"What are you doing?" Issa whispered. "We need to get out of here, not chit-chat."

"Trust me."

"Diet. Hmph. I don't have much choice here, now do I?"

Clip hopped off Issa's shoulder and moved down to Aboo so he could see the dragon better. "Not down here, no. In our world though, you can eat all you want. They have all sorts of great stuff."

"Really?" The dragon sat back on its haunches and peered up at the bird. "Like what?"

"All sorts of things! Ice cream, fruit cakes, cookies, and jellies."

"Ehhhh." Disappointment laced Storm Tist's voice. "All they have is vegetarian?"

"No, not at all. We have pepperoni pizza, it's my favorite," Luke chimed in.

Aboo nodded and added his own suggestions. "Fried chicken is amazing. Then there are barbeque ribs, hamburgers, stuffed pork chops, and steak. Oh, and bacon!"

"Yes, bacon!" Clip agreed. "You'd love it, I promise you."

Understanding their plan, she hoped, Issa adjusted her grip on the wall and peeked down to offer her own suggestion. "If you can help us escape, we'll take you back with us to the human world and give you as much meat as you want."

"That's the best offer I've had in a thousand years, and I've heard lots of offers. Come down, all of you, so we can talk."

"You won't eat us, right?" Aboo asked.

"I will not hurt you. Dragon's honor."

With nothing left to lose, the group climbed back down to the bottom of the pit. Luke sank to his knees, his limbs trembling from exertion. Aboo flopped down beside him, and Issa leaned her back to the wall. Clip glided over to Storm Fist's shoulder and took a perch.

"Will you really help us?" Clip asked.

"Why not? It's so dull in here and I can't even talk to the demons. They have poor taste and no manners whatsoever. I think I should like to be free of them. Now we just have to figure out how."

Chapter 18

Randy led Rick and Tamujin through the corridors. Everywhere they went in the demon palace looked the same, dark and grotesque. The deep bass of drums blended with discordant laughter in a chaotic symphony. The sound lifted the airs on Randy's nape and prickled his skin with goosebumps. He tried to ignore the eyeballs embedded in the walls, telling himself they were decorations only, and that they didn't really follow them as they moved down the hall.

"How did I ever let you all talk me into this?" Bones crunched beneath Randy's feet. He glanced downward and immediately regretted the action. A large, misshapen skull with rows of serrated teeth leered up at him.

"What's wrong? If you ask me, this is exactly your kind of place."

Randy cast a hateful look at his brother. Tamujin ignored them both and consulted the pendulum again.

"We are close. We should find them soon."

Thundering footsteps from behind them cut off any further conversation. The three men ran and searched for a place to hide, but the passageway stretched on without end.

"Holy crap!" Randy risked a glance over his shoulder. "You got any dragon catchers in your arsenal, Tamujin?"

"No."

"Then run!"

Searing flames licked at their backs. The dragon gained ground, each step making the ground shake. Randy tripped over his own feet and struck the stone floor. Rick, earing is pained grunt, skidded to a halt and doubled back. As the dragon opened its massive jaws to snap Randy up, Rick pulled his small back-up weapon and fired at the beast.

"Get up Randy! Don't make me regret coming back for you." He offered his free hand to his brother and pulled him to his feet while the dragon pawed its bullet-stung snout.

Side by side the two brothers ran for their lives with the dragon hot on their heels. They caught up with Tamujin but escape seemed far off.

They had reached a dead-end.

This is it. This is really it. I'm gonna die down here for nothing, Randy thought as they skidded to a halt. The dragon slowed now that its quarry was trapped. The scaled beast spat a jet of flame at the trio.

"That will be all, Thunderfoot. Good girl."

Gengir Xul's chilling voice filled them with dread. The sorcerer stepped out from a newly opened door with a retinue of demon soldiers behind him. He caressed a hand over the dragon's head.

"But Master," the dragon whined.

"Ah ah ah. No arguing, pet. Now, go catch yourself a rat or something. Our Lord is expecting his guests."

Thunderfoot stomped off in a huff. At Gengir Xul's behest the demons grabbed the three men. They marched them through the castle then shoved them into a chamber lit by a hundred candles in skull holders.

There, seated upon his throne, they saw Lord Shabalis for the first time.

Shabalis chuckled darkly. "What have we here? Three tender, juicy souls. How foolish of you to venture into my domain."

"I never asked to be here," Randy pointed out.

"Look at him, Xul. This one has potential. Think of the things he can accomplish."

Randy paused. "Potential for what?"

"To become a demon, of course. Your natural, dark talents would be greatly appreciated among us," Shabalis said.

"Everything that makes you an outcast in your world is an asset here," Gengir Xul said. He smiled. "The things that make others disdain you are what we look for in this world. Don't you want to fit in and feel as if you belong?"

"Really?" Randy asked.

"I see darkness in your soul. Anger, hatred… You definitely belong here," Shabalis agreed. His dark chuckle concerned Randy, but that was a small, insignificant point.

"Put him to a test, Master," Gengir Xul suggested.

"An excellent idea. We could use some entertainment," Shabalis said.

The inscription of a huge pentagram decorated the floor. As Shabalis raised his hands in the air and turned his palms toward the floor, it twisted and opened to reveal a bottomless, dark chasm. Howls and screams of tortured souls rose toward them, echoing from within.

Curious demons crowded over the edge of the pit, pushing each other to have a better look. Losing his balance, one toppled in, tumbling forward into the dark aether. His terrified wail was the last thing Randy heard, and then the creature was swallowed by the dark force dwelling within.

"Welcome to hell," Shabalis announced. "I know you are dying to do it yourself, Xul."

Cackling with insidious laughter, Gengir Xul grabbed Rick and shoved him over the edge. The detective grabbed onto the ledge and dangled over the chasm for dear life.

"Your brother is about to die the most horrible death," Shabalis said. "How do you feel about that, Randy?"

As if fixed where he stood, Randy gazed into Rick's terrified eyes. All of his hatred, resentment, and envy mixed with triumph. Years of loathing for his brother manifested in the expression on his face. For that moment, he was as hideous as the demons surrounding him.

"I feel good, actually."

"That's my boy," Shabalis said in an approving tone.

Without warning, a massive tentacle slithered up the rocky wall of the chasm. It wrapped around Rick's leg and pulled as the desperate man struggled to keep his hold.

"Randy, don't do this! Help me! You're my brother, remember?"

"Did you remember we were brothers when you put me behind bars?"

"Of course. I had nightmares about it, all these years."

"Me, too. Go to hell."

Shabalis aimed his sinister grin at Rick. "I think your brother will pass. Darkness wins and triumphs over all."

"It always does, doesn't it?" Gengir said.

"Are you going to stand here and watch your brother die?" Tamujin asked.

"He would do the same," Randy said. "He left me to rot in a damned prison for years because of his screwed up sense of morals. My own brother. My flesh and blood did that to me."

"This isn't about what he did then. This is about now, Randy. He saved your life on our way here. He pulled you back over the ledge when he could have let you go. That's what brothers do for each other. Help him," Tamujin implored with hope in his voice. "Don't do this and regret it for the rest of your life.

Randy's face softened. Rick may have locked him up, but at least he'd been alive. And in a way, locking him up had saved him from having to pay off those loan sharks. They would have busted his knees and put him at the bottom of the Pacific once they found him.

"Don't do that, Randy. Think of what we can give you," Gengir said.

"I must. He *is* my brother," Randy replied.

Gengir sighed. "We've lost him, Master."

"Not yet."

Randy tugged on one of Rick's hands with all of his strength. Sweat beaded over his brow, and Rick's hand, clammy and damp, began to slip between his fingers despite the effort he exerted.

"Stop. I can give you everything you have ever desired: riches, glory. I like you. You have a great talent. You can rule by my side," Shabalis said.

"What?" Gengir Xul straightened. A look of alarm crossed the dark sorcerer's features. "He can't take my place.

"Why not?" asked Shabalis. His cruel, calculating smile implied otherwise. He was the master of his domain and would do as he pleased regardless of the pain he caused to others.

"But Master—" Gengir began.

Shabalis cast a hard look at his pawn. The sorcerer quieted, but appeared to remain on edge and uncertain of his future. "This is not the time to debate your use, and had you proven yourself to be of greater worth to me, perhaps we would not be in this situation." His attention returned to Randy. "You can have and do anything. No restrictions, no ethics, no bullshit. Do you not want this?"

Randy hesitated for a fleeting moment.

"I'm giving you a chance to reach your full, dark potential."

"And be damned forever," Tamujin said.

Randy snapped out of it, and with a shout, he pulled Rick up with all of his might to drag him from the pit. Side by side, the brothers turned to face the horde of demons. All hell was soon to break loose, but at least they had each other.

"I'll probably regret this," Randy said.

Rick shook his head. "No, you won't. I'll make it up to you."

Shabalis rose from his throne. "Thunderfoot!" he called. At his cry for aid, a monstrous dragon entered the chamber. Dark scaled gleamed in the light, the color of an oil slick stretched over a moving mountain of reptilian muscle. Her huge maw opened to reveal rows of sickle-shaped teeth. And fire.

Stormfist, the other dragon from the pit, raced into the chamber through another entryway. Issa, Aboo, Luke, and Clip bounced upon his back. "Thunderfoot, noooo!"

Thunderfoot stopped in her tracks. "Why not? Have you lost your mind?"

"They can take us away from here. We can be free, be together again, Thunderfoot."

Without a hesitations pause, Thunderfoot turned against her former allies. A mighty roar exhaled streams of fire from her open maw, cooking the nearest demons into lumps of charred meat. The scent of roasting bodies filled Randy's nose, a sickening smell despite the victory it brought to their group.

Using the distraction, Issa ran to Rick and threw herself into his arms. Randy diverted his attention from the kiss that followed.

"I'll never let you out of my sight again," he murmured, kissing her again.

"Am I under arrest?" Issa asked him.

"You could say that," Rick replied.

Randy cleared his throat. "No time for love yet. Let's kick ass and get the hell out of here."

Randy and Rick turned to face the oncoming wall of demons. They were so numerous that they seemed to be without end, a limitless and terrifying force. They tried to fight against the demons but they were outnumbered. Bolts of energy shot by Shabalis and Gengir Xul crossed the chamber, as returning volleys of fire were spit by the dragons. Clip hovered over Storm Fist's head.

"Get them, Storm Fist! Get them!"

Tamujin fought against five demons attacking him from all directions. Despite that, he was more than capable of holding his own against them by reverting to his most wild state. He became like a demon himself. With his beastly jaws opened wide, he roared and bit the closest attacker. His bleeding victim howled in pain and tried to escape the ferocious genie.

Aboo and Luke were surrounded by more attackers than Randy could count, but a sea of monsters were between them and hindering any chance he had of reaching them. The kids fought desperately until one of the monsters grabbed Luke, dug his claws into the boy's shoulders, and laughed.

"Randy! I wish to be a Power Ninja!"

"You got it kid, wish granted."

For the second time in his life, Luke transformed into a Power Ninja. Somersaulting into the air, he landed a kick into a demon's face. The space around him cleared. Meanwhile, Aboo raced up the stairs with enemies in hot pursuit. Demons followed and reached for him with sharply clawed fingers. As he put on a burst of speed, he bumped into Gengir Xul.

"Gotcha, you little wimp!" Gengir Xul lifted Aboo high in the air. His eyes lit up as if he were charging his power.

"Tamujin!" Aboo cried for help.

Tamujin heard his call and tossed the demon catcher across the room. Aboo grabbed it and points it at Gengir Xul, just as the beam shot from the sorcerer's eyes.

"Not so fast, you asshole," Aboo said.

The lightning beams were caught by the demon catcher. Crackling and sending out explosive shards of electrical power, they eventually succumbed to the might of the demon catcher and pulled the sorcerer into the trap. In a high falsetto voice, seeming too girlish for his masculine appearance, Gengir cried out.

"Oh, no!"

"Yessss!" Aboo cheered.

The sorcerer shrank and vanished, pulled by his own energy beam into the demon catcher. After a brief moment, he was no more. There wasn't any time to celebrate when they realized that Tanju was dying. The genies focused on the gleaming stone, its pulses seeming weaker by the moment. Its heartbeat was almost nonexistent.

"It's too late," Tamujin announced. "Tanju is dying."

"We're shit out of luck," Randy muttered. He glanced around and grumbled when he took in their surroundings. Tremors ran through the chamber, announcing the coming destruction. Coughing survivors among the demonic horde rose.

"We can still save it, if we hurry," Aboo said.

Randy frowned. "I have an idea."

"Oh no," Rick said. He sighed. Nothing sucked worse than Randy's ideas, and he had a long memory of them from their childhoods.

"It's nothing like that. Trust me," Randy said.

"It's hard."

It would be nice if he could trust me just once. Just once in his life I'd like to have some respect, Randy thought, disgruntled, but too worried over the events to fret over his brother for long. He turned to Shabalis. "Hey! You there!"

"Are you talking to me?" the Arch Demon asked.

"Who do you think I'm talking to? What's the matter with you? Have you ever had your IQ tested?"

"No. What's IQ?"

"Obviously not," Randy muttered. "Never mind. We want to trade."

"You want to bargain with me?"

"You are slower than I thought. Forty, maybe fifty at the most."

"How dare you talk to me like that?" Shabalis demanded, rising taller.

"Because we have something you may want to exchange for the stone of Power."

"And what would that be?" Shabalis asked. The lord of demons raised one of his brows, a contemplative look over features. Good. They had his attention now.

"We captured Gengir Xul. We'll offer him back to you in exchange for Tanju," Randy said.

The mighty demon burst out laughing.

"Did I say something funny?" Randy asked.

"Keep him." Shabalis scoffed and made a dismissive gesture with one clawed hand, clearly disinterested in regaining control of his flunkie. Gengir was nothing more than a pawn to be used and disposed of once he exhausted his use. "I can find a replacement easily."

A noisy commotion arose from Aboo's pocket, emanating from the demon catcher. The small, distant voice of Gengir Xul rang with bitterness. Shabalis had deceived him well. "Huh? How could you betray me, Master? I have served you faithfully for centuries and more."

"Easily. You are the biggest moron I've ever met."

A strong tremor ran through the chamber, loosening rocks and debris. As dust fell and clouded the air, Tamujin glanced at the two humans. "We are wasting our time."

Issa lost her patience and stepped forward. "Stand aside, demon. We came to reclaim what's rightfully ours."

Without warning, Shabalis flicked his hand toward Issa and unleashed a volley of lightning. The bolt struck her dead center in the chest and seemed to hold her in its grasp. Her back arched and muscles all flexed rigid as electricity coursed through her body, igniting every nerve with pain. With a cry, she crumbled to the ground and was caught in the nick of time by Rick.

Seeing his opportunity, Clip flew over Storm Fist's head. "Get him, Storm Fist!"

The dragon exhaled a burst of fire toward Shabalis, blasting him with the intensity of a thousand blowtorches. Before the flame reached its destination, Shabalis vanished into thin air. Meanwhile, Tamujin raised his head after examining Issa. He knelt beside her very still and motionless body where she remained in Rick's arms.

"She is dead. There is nothing we can do, I'm afraid."

"No!" Rick cried. "There must be a way to bring her back. Tamujin, do something. You are a genie."

"Even a genie lacks the power of life over death," Tamujin said sadly. Tears shone in his eyes as he removed his palm from Issa's brow. "There's only one chance."

"Tanju! Tanju can help her. Let's go," Clip said.

They only had one chance, and they had to make it count.

"Follow me," Thunderfoot said. "I will lead the way!"

The massive dragon led the way, using her fiery breath to clear the passage ahead of them, killing any demons in their path.

By the time they reached the chamber, it seemed almost too late. Shabalis stepped from the shadow holding the stone of power. The post that once held Tanju was empty. They were far too late.

"Give it to me," Rick growled.

The Arch Demon Shabalis rocked with laughter so great it shook his entire body. "Don't worry about the girl. You'll soon be joining her."

Rick launched himself at Shabalis. His opponent launched lightning from his fingertips in an attack that would have caused Rick instant death. To his own surprise, Randy leapt between his brother and the monster with his demon catcher outstretched to intercept the beam. The talisman took the beam captive, along with the struggling demon on the other end of it. Struggling all the while to escape, Shabalis shrank and disappeared within the trap with Tanju.

"What have you done?" Rick demanded. "Now we've lost Tanju!"

"Some gratitude from a brother," Randy grumbled. "It was either take action or let your dumb ass die. Sorry for caring enough to save you.

Rick slumped on the ground next to Issa. He lowered his head in resignation. She was gone, and he'd never see her again.

Suddenly, a coughing sound echoed from the catcher's jewel. Seconds later, the strange magical item choked and spit Tanju out. The stone of power rolled across the ground, glittering vibrant rays of color. Tamujin beat Rick to it and plucked it up. The moment he touched the stone, he transformed into a handsome man, bearing his true appearance once more and no longer an ugly monster. He touched his face in amazement with one hand until Rick knocked the jewel from his hand and rushed with it to Issa's side. Instinct told him what to do, and he touched it to her lifeless heart.

Within seconds, the color returned to her face and she opened her eyes. A weak smile curved her lips. "Hey, you."

"Hey," Rick replied, holding her close.

"Hey, it's my turn now," Clip said.

A single touch from the gem transformed Clip to his natural appearance. He became a husky, seven-year-old boy. Tamujin hugged him.

"You should watch your diet, Clip, or shall I call you by your real name?"

"Badur works. Either way, I'm starving right now. I actually worked up an appetite for once."

"Me too," Randy agreed. Running from demons and infiltrating their evil lair had him famished. He couldn't imagine going any longer without food in his belly.

"Oh no!" Issa cried. "Look at Tanju!"

The Stone of Power seemed dead. Its inner light dimmed until it became a lifeless and dull piece of rock.

"It gave the rest of its life force to us, and now everything is lost," Tamujin said sadly. He looked regretful. His handsome and true looks came at too high a cost. At least he'd been human and alive, unlike Clip and Issa.

The sound of the collapsing citadel brought them back to reality. A big crack appeared in the ceiling and the chamber began to cave in. They ran as quickly as possible, rushing through one room to the next in the large castle. Without stopping, they burst onto the shaft and raced across the precipice. It shuddered and finally gave once all but Randy had crossed.

It happened in slow motion for him, the unstable ground beneath his feet one moment and gone in the next. He flailed at nothing, seeking to grab something, anything to help pull himself up and survive.

"Shit!" Randy cried as his body slammed into the rocky wall and he clung to the ledge. His fingernails scraped over the stone and began to slip. Fortunately, Tamujin and Rick were able to pull him up with ease this time.

"We have no time to waste! We must keep moving!" Issa shouted to them.

She was right. They had no choice but to keep going.

Randy's lungs burned for air, but stopping would mean his death, and he was too much of an ornery survivor to risk his life now. He'd been too much to give in. He pushed himself and sprinted ahead. Dust clung to his sweaty skin, dulling the gloss of the salty residue that burned his bleeding cuts.

With the others, he rushed through the gate at top speed. Being in shape had finally paid off.

"Excuse me!" the Guardian interrupted.

They all stopped in their tracks to appraise him. As his chest heaved, Randy swiped his forearm over his brow to remove a trickle of sweat seeping into his eyes.

"What is it?"

"You mentioned a career opportunity. Do you think there may be an opening?"

Randy and the others exchanged cautious glances. No one voiced their opinions on the matter.

"Take me with you," the Guardian pleaded.

More time passed, precious seconds of indecision ticking by to cost them time. Randy sighed. "Sure. Come on, buddy."

The rock rumbled and groaned as if stone scraped against stone. Eventually, a massive shape emerged from the sheet of jagged granite. It was bulky, muscular, and as hideous as Tamujin's cursed form. The ugly visage of the Guardian glowered at them and shook dust off his body.

A startled voice rang out into the chamber. "Wait! You can't leave your post, you're the Guardian."

"I quit," the big figure said.

By afternoon, the seven genies and their human friends had all assembled on the grass lawn in front of the mansion. They stood bathed in the bright, California sunlight, its golden yellow rays illuminating their tired faces. Once they gathered in a semi-circle, they all placed their hands over Tanju. The once radiant stone of power seemed dull and dark, lacking even the most basic spark of life.

For all of their work, it appeared they had failed. Randy watched from a distance with his arms crossed against his chest.

"At the beginning, there was Light," Abdul recited. "It dispersed the darkness, and brought life. I call upon the Power of Light to give Tanju a gift of life."

Glorious solar rays seemed to focus on Tanju, condensing into golden shafts of powerful light that bathed the lifeless jewel with warmth. Little sparks appeared first in the clear stone, swirling and growing stronger by the second. The genies continued to focus and concentrate on their task without showing a change in their expressions or breaking formation. Suddenly Tanju seemed to burst with a blinding brilliance.

Randy turned his face and shielded his eyes from the overwhelming explosion of light shining from the jewel. Its power washed over the mansion's yard, exuding a wave of heat that seared through Randy's skin. His flesh felt tight and hot afterward, long after the magical pulse of energy faded.

"It is done," Abdul murmured. The genies gazed reverently at the Tanju. "It is restored."

They celebrated the rejuvenation of Tanju by returning to the living room. True to his word, Randy handed the vessels back to each genie and renounced his claim of ownership while Tanju's unnatural, magical luster pulsed beautiful light over the room. One at a time, they stepped forward to receive the items that were once their magical prison, and at the end, even Randy had to laugh.

"I can't believe I'm doing this."

Salima smiled warmly at him. Issa did, too.

"I knew your soul wasn't completely lost," Karim said. "How does it feel to have it back?"

"Feels terrible," Randy exaggerated. "How am I going to make a living without any skills? Nobody will hire me with my record. The only thing I can do now is go back to grave robbing maybe. There's always good money there."

"That won't be necessary," Abdul said.

Randy glanced over at Rick and Issa. They held each other in a close embrace. *Sure, it won't. As usual, Rick gets everything and I get the shaft. He's got the girl and I'm back to being broke and worthless. I should have known it would end up this way,* Randy thought sourly. He tried to put on a smile to conceal how much the events had shaken his confidence but failed miserably.

"Rick got his girl, you all got your freedom. What did I get?"

"You received what's most important," Salima said.

"And what's that?"

"A family!" Karim shouted. On his words, the seven genies all converged on Randy to hug and kiss him, friendlier in their freedom than they were as captives under his control. Even Issa kissed his cheeks as he tried to brush them all away and escape. Eventually, his efforts weakened and he caved, allowing Salima to embrace him tightly in the way his mother never would. They all laughed.

I guess I do have a family now. Randy cracked a smile and laughed with them.

"We have something else to show you," Aboo said.

"What?" Randy asked.

Karim pointed to the television's current 900 line infomercial. Randy watched curiously as the hostess strut onto the studio's stage in her overpriced designer dress.

"We are proud to present our new and improved, 900 Master Wish Line. Through our exclusive screening process, we have selected best of the best, cream of the cream, to raise the quality of our service and bring it to a new level. Our 900 Master Wish Line is here to help you. Don't delay. Call now."

A montage of smiling faces transitioned by on the screen, conveying the ideal picture of happiness and wealth.

Randy watched curiously as the people all held up signs thanking 900 Master Wish Line for their current prosperity.

As the short video ended, the camera returned to the beautiful hostess. She flashed a Colgate smile to the viewers at home. "Remember, all it takes is a telephone and an open mind."

"I don't get it. Are there other genies I don't know about?" Randy finally asked.

Karim and his family members grinned. "Abdul, if you'll have the honors?"

Abdul conjured a glowing ball between his hands. The crystalline sphere emitted a gentle ivory light until finally an image appeared in its surface. Elsewhere, a thousand phones rang and rang. Voices whispered from the orb as Abdul used his power to make it hang suspended in the air like a mystical moon in Randy's living room.

In the pictured image, Shabalis, Gengir Xul, and a dozen demons field thousands of calls. They worked frantically to pick up the phone calls and grant petty wishes. Shabalis and Gengir Xul looked at each other in sorrow, almost weeping. "Nooooo!" they seemed to cry in unison.

"I wish... I wish... I wish..." The monotony continued, the perfect punishment for a horrific crime.

Randy clapped his hands and almost doubled over laughing. "That's great! What about the Guardian?"

The male genies in the group grinned while Issa and Salima shook their heads.

"Boys," Issa muttered under her breath, piquing Randy's curiosity.

"What? Is it something bad?"

"I will show you," Abdul said. As the image changed, its transitioning picture faded from the dismal call center to the bright banner of an UNDER NEW MANAGEMENT sign. The bold text was above the entrance to the Starlight Lounge — a nightclub. Nightclubs typically meant there were hot babes nearby, and that was always Randy's kind of place.

"You've definitely got my interest now," Randy said.

Issa rolled her eyes.

Johnny, also known as the Guardian of the Gate, stood by the entrance of the nightclub where he admitted patrons for the evening. A group of men in tailored suits entered and slipped Johnny a roll of bills as a tip. With their fancy shades and expensive clothes, they resembled modern day mobsters.

"That's more like it," Johnny said as he tucked the money away.

The scene in the crystalline ball changed, sweeping into the building to reveal the posh interior. Deluxe seating and booths with expensive purple and black-dyed leather stretched around an open floor beneath sensual mood lighting. A wall to wall aquarium held dozens of expensive marine fish from Hawaii, their yellow bodies gliding through the water amidst coral formations in vibrant colors.

Crush stood behind the bar, dressed in a suit and bowtie of exquisite style. He served drinks to bar patrons and poured pitchers of beer to the waitresses. At a closer glance, Randy saw the waitresses were ex-hookers and the prostitutes that he'd brought back to the house. They had new jobs now, legitimate women on the clock and earning fair wages. No more pimps and no more abuse from johns.

"Well, that's nice. I'm happy for him," Randy said.

"Oh, but wait," Karim said.

There was a stage with a heavy velvet curtain. It drew back to reveal a former hooker in a seductive cop uniform. She strutted up to the pole center stage and twirled her body around its spinning length. The show was on, and the crowd cheered as she performed a series of athletic maneuvers. The patrons rained money on her.

"I need to get there," Randy said.

"We all must go soon," Karim agreed.

"What about Tamujin? Where did he go? I could have sworn he was here a moment ago."

"Ahh... well..." Karim cleared his throat. "A moment would you."

He and Abdul moved closer to the ball and seemed to whisper. A moment later, they turned to regard Randy with smiles.

"We had to know it was an appropriate time to visit with Tamujin and Kimberly," Karim explained.

"Oh?" Randy's brows shot up higher.

The scene in the crystal ball changed again, revealing the interior of Kimberly's cramped home. The dog Floppy and his mate ran circles around a couple in a tender but thankfully very clothed embrace. They gazed into each other's eyes, expressions filled with affection and warmth.

"Hi, guys," Kimberly said.

"Hi," Randy said back to them. "We were just checking in. I didn't notice you were gone suddenly."

"Ah, yes. We chose to return to Kimberly's home. I'll be staying here from now on." He squeezed Kimberly close against him and she giggled in return. They were an adorable couple to watch and lightened Randy's spirits. Some of his bitterness and faded away. It wasn't so bad to see others enjoying their happiness.

"This place is really too small for us though," Kimberly said. "For all of us to be here anyway. Me, Luke, the dogs, and Tamujin can't fit here."

"Don't worry, Baby. I'm a genie. Would you like a palace? A castle perhaps? Just make a wish and I'll grant you whatever you desire."

When Kimberly turned her face up to Tamujin to kiss him, Abdul quickly dimmed the scrying crystal's view into their home.

"Hey, where's Aboo gotten off to?" Randy asked. "And Badur too?"

"Good question," Karim said.

Abdul waved his hands in a mystical gesture. Within seconds, a majestic view of the Earth and moon shone in the glowing orb's surface. The adults all stared at the image in confusion until Aboo, Badur, and Luke appeared on the flying carpet. They sped toward the far reaches of the solar system, laughing all the while.

"Luke!!! Luke!!!" Kimberly screamed.

"I'll be back, Mom!"